The NorthSide Clit

A Novel By

Allysha Hamber

To Sy,
Thanks for the love + support!
Allysha

Thanks for the love!
Allysha

THE NORTHSIDE CLIT®

THE NORTHSIDE CLIT

Written by: Allysha Hamber
Edited by: Dolly Lopez
Cover design by: Marion Designs/www.marion designs.com
Photos by: Marion Designs

Allysha Hamber

Lele4you@hotmail.com
Allysha4you@yahoo.com
www.myspace.com/allyshahamber
www.facebook.com/allyshahamber
www.twitter.com/allyshahamber
314-445-8034

Dedication

This book is dedicated to the most important people in my life, my children...Dorian Jones, Davion Hamber and Tamara Hamber. Please know that mommy loves all with everything inside me.

To my best friend Carlos Monterio Whitby...I miss you so much but I am so thankful, that your pain is now over. Rest In Peace for you are FINALLY FREE...I love you.

Acknowledgements

First and foremost I would like to thank My Heavenly Father for giving me the gift of writing. Without you, none of this would be possible.

To those who are dear to my heart, all my family and friends, I thank you all for your support.

A heart felt thanks to Alma Whitby. All my sisters from another mother, Jean Whitby, Shannon Rucker, Patricia Lyles, Simone Lowe and Sandra Mattox.

All my nieces and nephews, I love you all with all my heart. Stay close to each other throughout your lives together, nothing is more important than having a family that will love, guide, understand and support you, no matter what...

To all my fans who bought the first novel, I thank you for all your love and support! I will do my best to keep writing what you enjoy to read.

It All Began…

"Aey, Trey, lets bounce. We gotta go make this money. It's now or never, ya'll!" Queen yelled across the filthy parking lot of the Blue Meyer Projects. It was littered with empty beer cans, balled up cigarette packs, drug needles and everything else you could imagine. Graffiti representing gang signs were sprayed along the walls of the once beautiful duplex homes.

Built in the early 1970's, the public housing complex was now home to some of St. Louis' roughest patrons. The city that was once the beautiful gateway to the western part of the world was now ranked number one in violence and looked upon as the murder capital of the world. It was a tough place for young impressionable girls to grow and learn how to become women.

Queen held her hands up in the air to emphasize her point to the crew that she was all about chasing that paper and time was money. Her posse, known to the 'hood as the North Side Clit, had formed a little over four years ago as they came up on the grimy streets of North St. Louis. Inherited from their 'hood, their peers and their families, "gang banging" was deemed both a way of life and survival. The motto in the 'hood was simple, "Clique up or get fucked up!"

The North Side Clit was the baby project of its parent gangs, the North Side PG's and the North Side PGL's. The "Clit" was symbolic to the crew in a way that it represented the most sensitive and exciting part of a woman's body. No matter the size, a clit represents the gateway to the one organ on a woman's body known to bring a man, any man, to his knees.

Natasha Hudson, A.K.A. Queen, a native of the Blue Meyer Projects, initiated and formed the gang along with her buddies, Tranesha Simpson, A.K.A. Trey; Leslie Cain, A.K.A.

Butter; Arnelle Williams, A.K.A. Lilac; and LaShey Simpson, A.K.A. Pebbles. Each young woman brought their own style and their own vibe to the group.

Queen, the leader of the pack, was what some would call a twenty-one year old *'hood rat.* Many people misuse the phrase, but Queen was a *'hood rat* in the sense that, like a rodent, if you placed paradise at her feet, she'd opt to remain in the gutter. The 'hood was all Queen knew and it was the only place she felt comfortable and felt she belonged. She had respect in the 'hood and that made her feel important. It was the only place where she felt apart of something special.

Queen was thrown into the gang banging life style at an early age. Tagging along with her older brother, Sam, who was now doing time up state in Algoa Correctional Facility, along with some of her older cousins, as they "set it off" at banks, houses and liquor stores all over the metropolitan area.

She had already lost her younger cousin, Ryan, in a shootout earlier that year with the Mimika Mob on the city's north side. Her father was a typical dead beat and Queen had no idea if he were dead or alive. Her mother only spoke of him in anger and always in negativity. Queen's mother was an addict and over the years, had become heavily strung out on crack cocaine.

Standing at 5'6", Queen was always known as a bully to her peers. In the 'hood, kindness meant weakness, so she kept this protective shield around her at all times. She had a need to feel power--a need to never feel vulnerable.

Her hair was so long and beautiful but it was often hidden underneath the dark purple bandana she sported, and like the motto of *American Express*, "She never left home without it".

If you were smooth enough to get her to smile, she'd flash her Hawaiian gold with the letter "Q" carved inside.

"Why we gotta rush? You said ol' boy out of town, right?"

"The FreakNik is a three-day event, so what's the scurry?" Trey answered Queen as she lit up her favorite past time hobby, a Philly blunt. She inhaled the smoke slowly and deeply and she began to choke.

"Damn, this shit is the bomb, boo! Where did you cop this shit?"

Trey was a tomboy so to speak. She was an all-star basketball, softball and volleyball player at Vashon High School. With her skills shining in B-ball, she could've easily have been drafted to college and then to the WNBA. The offers poured in after her high school graduation but they often landed in the kitchen trash. Like Queen, Trey also believed that gutter living was the life for her and that no world existed outside of the "Lou."

Trey was a very attractive woman, a tantalizing 5'7" of pure buttery brown skin. Her high cheekbones showed her part Indian heritage. She always kept her shoulder-length silky hair braided up in the latest Allen Iverson styles. Her purple bandana was always sported underneath a fresh "314" or "STL" baseball cap. Her figure, though shapely, was always hidden under the latest sagging hip-hop gear.

Loyalty was Trey's middle name. She despised snakes. She gave loyalty and she demanded it tenfold in return. Her father, Wolf, one of The North Side PG's leaders, was set up by one of his own PG soldiers, causing him to spend the rest of his natural life behind the penitentiary walls. Because of that, Trey stayed cautious with whomever she came in contact with. She learned one thing to be true; a person can never hide whom they really are for too long.

All the fellas in the 'hood had mad respect for Trey. She was hard core, she was down to ride for her peoples, she was always ready to put in work, always ready to get on the grind, and she was gay. Everyone accepted Trey for *who* she was and not for *what* she was. She was not one of the "butch" women that tended to be a lesbian, trying to be a man. Trey was just being herself and the 'hood both honored and respected her for that.

Trey had often promised herself that she would one day leave the bangin' life and open up the first female owned barber shop in the St. Louis city. She was the best on the block at cutting hair. It was her dream, and some day she planned to pursue it. First though, she had to put those closest to her through college. It was something determined to do. And although not a bookworm herself, she pushed those closest to her to succeed in their education.

Trey's current lady was Butter, to whom she addressed her chronic induced question.

"I got it at the spot over on Page and Taylor. Lonnell, Bird and 'nem was out chillin' in the park when I rode through. I asked him was he good and he put me down."

Butter reached down inside the car and pulled out a brown paper bag. "Here, Boo. I stopped and brought you some shrimp fried rice and some orange chicken from Bing Lau's."

Trey Smiled.

"That's why I love you girl! You always lookin' out for your nigga ain't you, boo?"

Butter moved in closer to Trey and placed a knee between her legs.

"I'll always have your back, Trey, you know that. I'm the Bonnie to yo' Clyde, nigga." She leaned in closer and sent her tongue out to meet Trey's. Their lips locked and their tongues danced softly together.

"Come on, baby, let's go do some thangs."

"I'd love to but don't you and Queen gotta go and handle some business?" Butter asked. Trey leaned into her.

"Shit, baby! Ain't nothing mo' important than you, you heard me?"

Buttercup flashed her woman a smile that could melt the coldest heart.

Their relationship had grown so much closer since Trey moved Butter out of her grandmother's two-story public housing unit in The Jeff Vanderlou, one of the city's roughest projects, partly because Trey had so many enemies in the JVL's and partly because of Butter's Grandmother's opinion of their relationship.

Butter's grandmother, Mary, a sanctified soul saving Christian, didn't approve of her relationship with Trey. She verbally made her opinions known as she often told both Butter and Trey that their relationship was abomination unto God. For the life of her, Mary couldn't understand how her little Leslie had ended up in a gang, let alone a lesbian relationship with another woman. Mary often blamed herself for Butter's current situation. She felt that if she had not gotten sick and been forced to quit her job at General Motors, she could've kept Butter in the suburbs of O'Fallon, where little, if any gang bangin' occurred. Instead, she fell ill, lost her job and had to move Butter to one of the city's poorest and roughest neighborhoods.

"Can I roll with you?" Butter asked as Trey wrapped her arms around her waist.

"Naw, boo, you know better than that. You know I don't like you around nothin' I do dirty. You a good girl and you gon' stay that way."

"But..."

"No buts, baby. You goin' to college. I'm a see to that, you heard me? This *hurr,* this shit ain't for you, you better than this."

Trey kissed her softly on the forehead.

Butter was only 5'5", but had the heart of a giant. She was intelligent and bright, full of ambition and dreams. Trey knew Butter deserved a chance to really be somebody, even if it meant leaving her behind and getting out of the "Lou".

"Well, just be careful, okay? I want you to promise me you'll be safe."

Trey ran her fingers up Butter's thighs, moved her panties to the side and entered inside her with her middle finger. Butter looked around to see if anyone was watching them. Honestly, she didn't care. The openness of their relationship to the public turned her on tremendously. Most lesbian couples downplayed their affection for one another out in the streets, afraid of what people might think or say, but Trey always let the world know that she loved her woman and didn't give a fuck what anybody said about it. Because of that, Trey was Butter's world and she loved the way Trey made her feel.

"Umm, why you so wet? Missed me?"

"Always, Trey. You know that."

Butter swung her right leg around Trey's waist, propping her foot up on the front door of Trey's dark gray Short Dog Caddy. Her body gyrated against Trey's fingers as Trey moaned in her ear, "You love me?"

"You know I love you, Trey."

"You got my back, down fo' whatever?"

"Always, Trey."

Trey's system bumped out the sounds of Jahiem's *Ghetto Love.*

"*…Stop frontin', it's time to give a nigga what he want and you know I got that fever, don't you want it? While I'm lickin' on your lips and rubbin' on yo' thighs. You got me tempted, so fine at times you gotta a nigga trickin'…*"

Butter's head went back and the sweetest moan escaped through her lips as she enjoyed Trey's intrusion inside her. "Ohh, Trey…!" Butter's body gave every indication that an orgasm was near, only to be interrupted by the sound of Queen's commanding voice, demanding for the crew to assemble.

"Damn, she tripping'!" Trey said, frustrated as she removed her hand from underneath Butter's skirt.

Butter reluctantly dropped her leg and kissed Trey softly and teasingly on her lips. "Go handle yo' business, baby. I'll be waiting up at home for you later."

Trey told her to drive the car home and not to go to sleep until she got there. She hit Butter on the ass and said, "Don't start without me."

Trey stood and watched Butter climb into the car and adjusting her silk panties between her thighs. "You got me all sticky and shit. You know I hate that."

Trey smiled. "Quit frownin' up and quit actin' like you don't like it."

When Butter drove off, Trey strolled over to lock up with Queen, Pebbles and Lilac.

"What's good pimpin'?" Pebbles asked, slapping Trey on her arm.

"It's yo' world, lil' momma. I'm just a squirrel tryin' to get a nut."

"So I see, with yo' nasty ass," Pebbles teased, nodding towards Grand Avenue as Butter turned the corner.

Trey took the fingers she removed from inside Butter and placed them slowly inside her mouth. She twirled her tongue around each of them, licked them and then smiled. "UMMM, just like butter, baby! Finger lickin' good!"

Pebbles punched Trey in the chest.

"Damn, nigga! That shit is gross! Quit that shit. I don't like pussy, I'm strictly dick-ly."

"So you say," Trey teased.

"So I know," Pebbles stated.

Trey and Pebbles were first cousins and grew up in the same high-rise complex of the Blue Meyers. When Pebbles' mother went to prison five years earlier for trafficking drugs, Pebbles moved in with her grandmother and Trey. Pebbles looked up to Trey regardless of Trey's sexual preference. It didn't matter because in Pebbles' eyes, Trey had it goin' on.

Pebbles sometimes saw the soft and gentle side of Trey that she kept hidden from the rest of the world, including Butter. It was a sensitive and warm side of Trey. Everyone thought that Trey was too overprotective of both Pebbles and Butter, but only Pebbles knew of the nights Trey sat up with her, holding her tightly when she cried for her mother. Trey had been there for her and Pebbles loved her unconditionally for that.

For the life of her, Pebbles couldn't understand why Trey pushed her so hard--so hard, to be better than everybody else. Pebbles was the youngest of the crew at the age of eighteen and she was the only one still in high school, set to graduate later that year.

"Ya'll ready to roll or what?" Queen asked, pounding her right first into her opposite hand.

"You know I'm with it," Trey spit out, checking her nine-millimeter clip and placing it down inside her waist in case of trouble.

"Me too," Lilac joined in.

"I'm game," Pebbles said as she placed a stick of Double Mint gum in her mouth.

"Like hell you game! Yo' ass ain't goin' no where but home. Now get to steppin'," Trey pressed.

Pebbles stepped back, placed a hand on her hip and snapped her neck. "Fuck that, Trey. I deserve to come up just like everybody else. I need shit just like everybody else. Why I always gotta be left out of shit? I mean, you my peeps and all, but damn that, I'm rollin'."

Trey looked at Pebbles with her head cocked to the side and chuckled to herself. She had always taught Pebbles to stand up for herself and hold her ground against any and everybody if she believed she was right. However, in Trey's eyes, this time she was wrong. Pebbles wasn't thuggish like the rest of them. She wasn't built for street drama. But Trey also realized that she wasn't a baby anymore and she had to let Pebbles find her own way, even if it meant by trial and error.

Truth be told, she admired the courage Pebbles had just shown, and although it was against her better judgment, Trey stood down. And while she knew she had to let Pebbles grow up sometime, she didn't like her around any of their illegal activities. Trey just didn't feel Pebbles was ready.

"A'ight, big timer, but don't freeze up and shit if somethin' jumps off."

Pebbles, in her best mid-western accent said, "Nigga, I'm from the Show-Me-State. I don't talk about it, I be about it."

Queen jumped in the driver's seat of her midnight blue 1985 Chevy Impala and yelled, "A'ight then, lets go make this money."

The crew piled into the car and lit up blunts simultaneously as they cruised to the sounds of Nelly. "*...You can find me in St. Louis rollin' on dubs, smokin' on bud in clubs, blowing up like Cocoa Puffs...*"

Trey laid back, stared out the window at the neighborhood and began reassuring herself that this job, like all the others, would go off without a hitch. She felt a tinge uncomfortable with Pebbles riding along and tried not to think about it as the crew hit Interstate 70 West and headed out to St. Charles. This job was deemed an easy mark, but what they would soon find out is that no job, no matter how big or small, was all that easy.

Chapter One

"**A**'ight, check it," Queen announced as she turned off the radio, making sure she had everyone's attention.

"This nigga we about to hit is worth mad cheddar. I hear he's the head-nigga-in-charge of the St. Louis Rams and he's bankin', you feel me? He stay out here in St. Charles right off the lakefront. The AmeriStar Casino sits about three blocks away from his crib. Here's the plan. We go in, we do our thang and then we hit the boat, a'ight? That gives us a place to hang out and chill until mornin' and let shit cool down."

"And you double checked and made sure he's gone to the ATL?" Lilac questioned Queen, fishing for some reassurance.

Lilac was the "cut-throat" of the crew. She obtained that brand name back in the day when she ran with the "Switch Blade Sistaz," carrying a box cutter where ever she went and using it to give her enemies a lasting memory of their conflict and brawls. Now, being seasoned in the game, Lilac could now talk effortlessly with a razor blade buried underneath her tongue.

The darkest of the crew, Lilac moved to the Blue Meyers during her junior year of high school. She was often picked on by rival crews because of her small 5'3" frame that carried only one hundred and twenty four pounds. Queen took Lilac under her wing, got next to her and protected her, not that Lilac needed it. Queen once watched as Lilac went toe-to-toe with a crew of four girls all by herself. Queen admired that in her because that meant she was strong and she could hold her own. That also meant that she could only *bring* game to The Clit, not take it away.

Lilac admired the respect Queen had in the 'hood and did all she could to prove herself worthy of being apart of the infamous crew. It was Lilac who did all the research on potential targets for the girls to hit. To date, she had found them some very prestigious targets that had brought very good profits. Yet, this would be their biggest job and Lilac was proud of herself for moving her game to the next level, although as always, Queen would get all the credit. Lilac didn't mind though, she was just glad to be apart of The Clit, since she had no brothers or sisters of her own.

The Clit was family to her and she'd lay down her life for them at any moment. She wore tattoos across her neck and back representing the 314 set she claimed. Despite her lovely looks, most of the fellas in the 'hood felt Lilac was too hardcore to date; hell most of them was afraid of her after watching her slice her foes damn near to pieces.

Lilac was a natural born hustler, peddling rocks in the 'hood and sharing her wealth with her single mother, Shirley, and her crew. She always had their backs. Tonight would be no different.

"Yeah, he's gone, I made sure. I checked with my connect before we bounced," Queen assured them.

What connect? Lilac thought to herself. *How the hell she check with a connect and I'm the one who found the job? Queen need to quit that shit!*

When they reached the corner of Felix Avenue, Queen cut the lights off and parked the Impala at the end of the block behind a black and silver Ford Expedition. A row of exquisite homes lay in front of them, huge mansions that were home to some of St. Louis' finest protégés. Lilac made a mental note to check out future marks along the street.

"A'ight, Lilac, you take the back. Trey, you cover the side and Pebbles, we'll take the front."

Trey put up her hand in protest. "Naw, naw, no can do, Queen. Pebbles is comin' with me."

"Trey, don't start trippin'. We both know that Pebbles can't hop through no damn window. Hell, she can't even hop right in simple damn game of hopscotch. But she can pick the hell out of any dead bolt lock you put in front of her and disengage any alarm system we may come across. You know she all brainiac with them electronics and shit. She's already here so you might as well let her earn her keep. Hell, if shit get twisted, she fallin' too, right?" Queen pushed.

Trey placed her blunt in the ashtray after taking one last hit. She contemplated Queen's theory. Pebbles was there and the front entrance to the house had a better view and a clearer pathway to the car Trey reasoned. "A'ight, but you stay yo' ass right beside her," she said to Pebbles.

"I got this," Pebbles insisted.

"A'ight, got this," Trey interrupted. "If any alarm sound, you get yo' ass back to this car pronto, you heard me?"

"Yeah, I hear you, momma," Pebbles answered sarcastically, placing a kiss on Trey's cheek. As always, she knew Trey was only looking out for her best interest.

Queen hit the hydraulics and the Impala came to rest only inches from the ground. They each put on their black skullies to cover up their purple bandanas and to match their dark clothing as they exited the car. It's pretty hard to identify four black people with black clothes on in the black of night.

After Lilac climbed to the top of the concrete wall and pulled the wire from the back of the security camera, The Clit hopped the metal gate at the entrance of the drive way one by one.

Trey branched off and proceeded to the side of the house followed by Lilac, who proceeded towards the rear.

Lilac passed a huge swan-shaped swimming pool along the way to the back. She frowned and shook her head in disgust. *Damn, that don't make no fuckin' sense! That damn thing is bigger than the one at Wohl's Neighborhood Center. Rich ass bastard! I ain't never heard of him donating a dime back to the 'hood. That's exactly why we finna clip his ass.*

On the side of the house, Trey found her point of entry. She chose a window that had a hefty stretch of grass underneath so she wouldn't leave any footprints behind. She stood on the top of a metal trash bin, awaiting her signal that it was safe to move in.

The gateway to the mansion was a beautiful set of black oak and marble mixed doors. Pebbles took out the shiny aluminum scalpel from her backpack and began to jimmy the lock. It wasn't budging. "Queen, look in the front pocket of my bag and give me that sack of pins."

With the triple team of the scalpel, pin and a card, Pebbles successfully popped the lock on the front door. Once the lock popped and the door opened, the girls braced themselves for the alarm but none came. Queen and Pebbles slapped a high five. "Yeah, now that's what I'm talkin' about!" Queen said as she hit Pebbles on the butt. "You one bad broad, lil' momma."

Queen took her hands and placed them to her mouth like a megaphone and began barking like a dog. That was Trey's signal to make her move. It was also a great disguise to nosey neighbors. After all, didn't dogs always bark all night over the littlest things?

Trey pulled her pocketknife from her blue jean Phem shorts and slid it underneath the latch of the metal bars the owner had installed for this very reason. The black iron gate popped open and

Trey swelled with pride. *Oh yeah!* She sneered as she slid up the window and hopped inside, landing in what appeared to be an office or den.

Quickly, Trey surveyed the room for a camera. She moved across the room to the mahogany and oak desk equipped with a computer, a pile of papers and a printer. Behind her stood a bookshelf made of the same chocolate covered oak. Trey began thumbing through the desk drawers, first turning up nothing of significance. She was looking for a key to unlock the safe her gut instinct told her was hidden inside that room. Trey always had instincts like a lion hunting for prey.

She continued to comb through the room, looking behind pictures, underneath lamps and behind art fixtures. Frustrated, she stood in the middle of the room and focused on the bookshelf. She walked over and began scanning through the books on the shelf, again relying solely on her instincts. The books' authors ranged from Shakespeare to John Gresham.

As Trey turned to leave, she noticed from the corner of her eye a small book nestled in the right corner of the third shelf. She reached for the tiny book titled *Dopefiend,* by Donald Goines. Trey flipped through the pages and out dropped a small gold key. She smiled to herself. Out of all those white authors, Donald Goines stuck out like sore thumb. *You thought you was smart, huh?*

••••••

Queen and Pebbles headed to the kitchen to unlock the back door for Lilac. Pebbles was in awe of the beautiful interior of the home. The paintings on the walls were so amazing to her. The kitchen was huge, with a white marble floor, a midnight blue dining set and matching midnight blue and white accessories.

There was skillet full of burnt fried chicken wings on the stove. Queen laughed and shook her head. "As rich as his ass is, I hope he hires a damn maid 'cause his ass cooks worse than I do."

"Right," Pebbles agreed. "And you know yo' ass will burn boilin' water."

They opened the door for Lilac.

"Aey, I'll check out the downstairs rooms. Ya'll can make it upstairs to the bedrooms," Lilac told them, pulling her duffel bag from underneath her black hoodie.

As Pebbles and Queen walked out, Lilac began searching the kitchen drawers for anything of value. From experience, she knew that most rich white folks kept their most expensive jewelry in safes. But for some strange reason, rich black folks tended to hide theirs in the freezer. *Like thieves don't steal frozen meat!* she chuckled.

She headed to the refrigerator after emptying all the sterling silverware into her duffel bag. She spotted some crystal wineglasses and quickly placed them down in an inside pocket of the duffel bag. *I'll give these to moms.*

Lilac opened the freezer and emptied all the contents on the floor. Pissed that nothing was there, she went into the living room and began dismantling its contents. When she turned up nothing worthwhile, she headed over to the den. Trey was standing by the bookshelf with a small gold key in her hand.

"You got somethin'?" Lilac asked.

"I got the key, I'm sure of it, but I can't find the fuckin' safe. I know it's in this room somewhere."

Lilac began to scan the walls as Trey had done before. Her eyes landed on a framed self-portrait of whom she assumed was the owner of the house. He looked young. *Maybe he was the heir to the throne.*

"Did you check behind here?"

Lilac walked over to the picture, set her bag down and stared at the portrait. "From what I hear, he's an arrogant son-of-a-bitch. So what better place to hide yo' grip than behind a shrine of yourself?"

Lilac removed the picture from the wall and, sure enough, there was the safe they'd come for mounted in the wall.

Trey ran over and slapped Lilac on the back. "Way to do the damn thang, girl! Time to set it off."

Trey placed the key in the lock, turned the handle and opened the safe. "Oh yeah!" Trey said as she opened the door. Their eyes damn near popped out of their heads. "Oh shit! Look at all that loot!" Lilac screamed. She jumped up and down as Trey removed the stacks of money from the safe. Each stack was laced with a hundred-dollar bill on top.

"Damn!" Trey said, stuffing the stacks in her backpack. "There's gotta be damn near a hundred gee's in here!"

"We rich, nigga! We filthy fuckin' rich!" Lilac shouted. Doing her best Vivica Fox impression, she grabbed one of the stacks and kissed it. "Now that's how you set it off!"

••••••

As Queen and Pebbles chose which room to search at the top of the hallway, Queen chose the bedroom on the left and Pebbles took the one on the right further down the hall.

When Pebbles entered the bedroom, her eyes lit up. *Damn, this nigga must be filthy!* The furniture was made of black oak and marble, with smoked mirrors lining the walls and the carpet a plush snow-white. It set off the black and white comforter set on the bed.

Queen's mind echoed Pebbles' thoughts as she opened the doors to the spacious walk-in closet. *Damn, this is butta!* she muttered to herself as she entered the closet that was bigger than her entire bedroom at home. The owner's suits were all aligned by colors, coordinated by texture and separated by their name brands--Versace, Sean Jean, Ralph Lauren, Gucci--.the names went on and on.

To her left were shelves and shelves of shoes--alligators, snakeskin, running shoes, Air Force One's and Nike's of every color, Timbs, Lugz and Fubu boots out the ass. He had it goin' on, she had to admit.

She searched behind the clothes for a wall safe but came up empty. She moved back into the bedroom and began picking through the drawers of his white marbled chest. Everything was folded so neatly; socks rolled and matched by colors, underwear pressed and folded, condoms neatly stacked in the corners.

Queen laughed. "I ain't never seen a nigga this neat. Shit, even his jimmies is color coordinated!" She chuckled again as she picked up a Trojan and read the label, "Edible Magnums". "Edible? Fuckin' pervert!" She returned the condom to its place.

Trey and Lilac came storming through the bedroom door, causing Queen to jump. "Bitch, ya'll scared the shit out of me!"

"Yo, we got what we came for. Lets bounce," Trey told her.

"A'ight, hold up a sec. We got all night and I know this nigga got jewelry, rocks and shit up in here. By the way, Trey, you like wearing all that masculine shit. You need to check out homie's closet. He got mad shit in there," Queen said, pulling open another drawer.

"Yo, forget that shit. We didn't come for all that, we got the cash so let's be out!"

Lilac looked at Trey and sat her bag down on the floor and began to help Queen search the room. With Lilac, it was whatever Queen wanted. "Come on Trey, it'll go faster if we all look."

Trey shook her head. Queen was getting too greedy.

"Yo, ya'll trippin'. We came to get money, we got it, now its time to get ghost."

"Chill, fool! You always buggin' and shit" Queen said as her eyes smiled down at the diamond Rolex watch she'd just discovered underneath a stack of wife beaters in his bottom drawer.

"You happy now? You got bling. Can we go now?" Trey insisted, picking up her bag from the floor. As she walked out the room, she heard a door close downstairs.

"Yo," she said, storming back into the room. "I thought you said this mark was gone 'til Sunday!"

"He is," Queen assured her.

"Well, that better be Pebbles going out that damn door I just heard."

"Oh shit!" Lilac said as she looked out the window of the bedroom, noticing how high off the ground they were just in case jumping was an option. It was not. "Damn, ya'll! What we gon' do?"

"Shit, I don't know what ya'll gon' do, but I'ma blast that muthafucka if I have to!" Trey said, pulling out her nine millimeter from the back of her waist.

The surround sound of the television clicked on and Trey cocked back the handle on her Glock.

"While he got the TV on, we can sneak past him. Let's get Pebbs and get the fuck outta here!" Queen said, charging through the door.

They shot over to the next bedroom. There was no sign of Pebbles. They checked the upstairs office down the hall, still no Pebbles.

Trey was getting more and more frustrated by the second. "Where the fuck is she? Queen, I told you to keep her right beside you, damn!"

"I tried," Queen lied. "But she wanted to do her own thang."

Trey looked at Queen and frowned. "Now you see why I didn't want her ass here with us. What if she's downstairs some fuckin' where?"

Finally, Lilac threw her hands up, pleading with Queen and Trey to leave.

"Pebbles ain't dumb. Maybe she heard the door close and she split. Now, I ain't about to stand here and risk five to ten searchin' for a muthafucka who ain't here."

Queen agreed. "Yeah, you probably true. She probably on her way to the car wondering what the hell is takin' us so damn long," she said.

Trey was hot as fish grease by now. She un-cocked the Glock and returned it to her waist, mumbling that for their sakes, they'd better be right. If anything was to happen to Pebbles, she'd never forgive herself or them. "A'ight then, lets be out."

They went back into the second floor hallway and peeped down over the rail. They couldn't see anyone. Slowly, they started creeping down the stairs, sliding their backs against the wall. All three were sweating bullets, hoping not to run into the owner. Once they reached the bottom of the steps, they could slide across the kitchen to the door and they'd be home free...or so they thought!

Chapter Two

Xavier Winston had been a resident of Saint Louis since he was born in 1973 at Homer G. Phillips Hospital. He was raised in the Peabody Projects in the city's downtown ghetto. He attended O'Fallon Technical High School, graduating with an upper 3.0 grade point average. He always had a love for football, playing little league at the local Herbert Hoover Boys Club on Grand Ave. He played high school ball and had received an offer to play at Mizzou College until he tore his ACL in the homecoming game against their rival, Sumner High School, in his senior year.

Xavier was a very handsome 6"2', caramel-colored man. His hair, dark and wavy, was cut down low, connecting to his neatly lined beard and goatee. His shoulders were broad, his arms muscular, and his abs and thighs were cut from working out.

He was always popular. Women craved Xavier and he treated them according to his mood that particular day. He hung in the 'hood with the local gang, selling boy (heroin) and cocaine on the side as a hustle to support his habits--shopping and women.

The drug game has definitely been good to me, he thought to himself as he stood in the living room, staring at his one hundred eighty thousand dollar home he had built from the ground up. He had hustled his way to the top, becoming a millionaire, investing his drug money into prospering businesses such as Xavier's Liquor & Grocery, Winston's Pawn & Jewelry, along with his most intelligent investment to date--stock in the Saint Louis Rams football team and their new stadium. The investment would pay off well, better than he could've ever dreamed.

The game had made him rich enough to be legit. So why wasn't he? He still used the streets to stack his bank accounts and feed his thirst for the street life. He'd long ago stopped dealing with the small town hustlers. Now Xavier only dealt with the big boys, brothers and Colombians with clout and the cash to back it up. His businesses offered him the perfect front, which kept the Feds off his back.

To anyone on the outside looking in, Xavier had it all. But only Xavier knew the sadness he felt when he was alone at night. He still grieved the loss of his young and beautiful wife, Stephanie, who died while giving birth to his son. She had been his woman long before he'd gotten big in the game and Xavier knew she was blue. She loved him for who he was, not what he could give her. That was rare, if not unheard of in the game. Money or not, Stephanie insisted on making her own income, paying her own way and standing on her own two feet. That's what he loved so much about her. She wasn't like the others, gold diggin' and moochin' off any and every man they thought their pussy could seduce.

A complicated delivery had stressed the baby in Stephanie's womb. His heart rate dropped dramatically low, so the doctor ordered Stephanie to undergo an emergency cesarean to save the lives of both mom and baby, but they both died on the operating table. The labor was premature and Xavier was out of town on business. The last time he'd see his wife and the first time he'd see his son would be on a cold, steel table in the morgue.

He ordered a specially made double casket at Wade's Funeral Home. He wanted to have them buried side-by-side, mom holding baby in her arms.

The loss was more than he could handle. Business froze, clients panicked and Xavier sank deep into depression. He couldn't see his future without them, mostly from the guilt he felt inside for not being there we they needed him most. He'd left the master bedroom and nursery exactly the way Stephanie had it the day she died. Xavier moved into a second bedroom because he couldn't stand to sleep in their bed without her.

He stood over the end table, staring at the two tickets to Atlanta he had bought a week earlier. He'd purchased one for Sasha, his on again-off again girlfriend.

It was Xavier and Stephanie's five-year anniversary today. He planned to fly down to Atlanta and visit the place they married, though this was unknown to Sasha. Xavier wanted once again to pledge his love eternally to Stephanie, but he changed his mind at the airport. He couldn't go through with it. He felt guilty for even being with another woman at times, let alone having one accompany him to their special city of love. Xavier made up an excuse about being ill, dropped Sasha off and headed back home. He just wanted to spend a quiet night alone with his thoughts.

Xavier turned and walked around to the back hallway of the house. The walkway passed along the wash room, garage entrance and den--thankfully only one of the places the girls had searched, and Trey, unlike Lilac, didn't ransack the place.

He climbed the stairs and entered the nursery Stephanie was working on the day she died. It was painted baby blue and white with Mickey and Minnie Mouse, and Donald and Daisy Duck across the walls. He glanced at the tiny white crib, still unassembled over in the corner. He inhaled deeply, fighting back the tears he felt rising within him. *What good is all this if you have no one to share it with? No one to leave it to. God, I miss you Steph!*

No one has ever seen Xavier cry. On the outside, he was tough as nails. The streets greatly respected Xavier, although he would never consider himself a gangster. He was just a man, a Black man who did what he had to do to survive. His motto about life: "*Trust no one, but try everyone*".

The only person Xavier felt he could trust with his life was now gone. The one he'd someday groom to take over his empire was also gone. No doubt he could've knocked up women on a regular, but he made a promise to Stephanie when they married.

"Xav, I want to you to promise something," Stephanie said, lying in his arms after making love to him for the first time as husband and wife.

"Anything for you, you know that."

"Promise me that no matter what you do out there in the streets, you won't bring it into our home. What I mean by that is this; I'm no fool, Xavier. I know what goes on out there. The groupies, the tricks and the gold diggers. Promise me that no matter what, you won't share the bond of having a child with anyone except me. That's all I ask."

Stephanie had never asked Xavier for anything. The money, cars, jewelry, none of it phased her. She only wanted him, so, Xavier had no problem granting the love of his life this special wish.

He reached in his pocket and pulled out his prescription bottle of Paxil and popped one to help calm his mood. He then went out into the hallway and he noticed the white oak door to the master bedroom was slightly ajar. This was unusual because he kept that door locked at all times. Even Thelma, his maid, knew to lock the door after cleaning.

Instinctively, he drew his forty-five semi-automatic. He quickly cocked back the handle and stood by the door, listening to the soft mumbling inside. Xavier was trying to make out how many people were on the other side of the door.

••••••

Pebbles stood in disbelief, staring at all the beautiful clothing hanging in the spacious closet. Furs, minks, leather and suede coats lined the left side. *Man!* she thought. *Just one of these is about a year's worth of paychecks for me!*

Pebbles ran her hand down the gray, floor-length mink coat. She'd never felt anything so soft in her life. She slowly moved down the rack, admiring the owner's beautiful taste in clothes. Her eyes rested on a leather, strapless, black mini dress. She glanced at the tag. Medium. It was her size.

Pebbles' intentions were to just try on a couple outfits, not steal them. She began to peel off her Apple Bottom jeans and T-shirt right there in the closet.

Xavier, noting the silence inside the room, slowly pushed the door with his gun drawn and stepped inside. Upon entrance, he didn't see anyone, but as he turned to his left, there she was. Her long silky black hair hung mid-way down her back, her caramel colored shoulders slightly slumped, as if she was carrying the weight of the world upon them. The deeply set in crease of her back was intriguing, attractive and it led to a plump, beautifully shaped butt that at a glance made Xavier's mouth water.

He watched as she slid on his wife's black leather mini dress. He'd purchased the dress for Stephanie on one of his many business runs. Xavier knew the moment he saw it on the rack, it was perfect for his wife. He watched the creature, though bold as she was, gracefully slide into the dress Xavier thought could only look so stunning on Stephanie. He was wrong.

Unaware of his presence, Pebbles turned around to face the full-length mirror off to the side of her. She was impressed. She took her right hand and flung her hair off her shoulders, creating an instant hard on for Xavier. He was in a trance, gun now lowered to his side.

"Damn, I look good in this! I wonder does she look as good as I do in this fly ass dress."

"She used to," Xavier quickly responded without thinking. Pebbles jumped back and instantly began explaining.

"I...I...was...I'm so sorry! Please don't shoot me! I wasn't gonna steal it...I was just..." She was nervous and stumbling for words.

"I'm not gonna shoot you, unless you make me," Xavier said un-cocking his gun. "But you are gonna tell me who the hell you are and what the fuck you doin' in my wife's closet!"

"I was...we was..."

Pebbles was interrupted by the sound of the house alarm. Xavier had reset the alarm on when he entered the house. The sound of the alarm made Xavier realize that he didn't encounter the alarm when he first entered the house. That meant Thelma didn't set it before she left for the weekend. *Was she in on this?*

He made a mental note to fire her ass bright and early in the morning. He once again drew his weapon and aimed at Pebbles. "When I get back, I swear you better be right there in that same fuckin' spot. Where's your ID?"

"In my back pants pocket."

"How many are downstairs," Xavier asked.

"I don't know."

Xavier cocked the handle. "Don't fuck with me. How many?"

"Three," Pebbles answered.

Xavier walked to her and bent down beside her. He could smell her. Her essence, her flavor...her love. He had to regroup. He removed her ID from her pocket and glanced at her name, LaShey Simpson.

Xavier placed her ID in his back pocket and headed down the stairs, stopping along the way to retrieve his nine-millimeter from a hallway drawer. His mind crept back to the beautiful creature in his bedroom. Her hazel eyes, her beautiful lips so full and pouty, her cheekbones resembling those of a Indian princess.

The footsteps and voices of his intruders quickly snapped him back to reality. He pulled out his cell phone and called the police, reporting intruders in his home. Although a Black man, Xavier was a rich ass Black man, so he knew the law would respond quicker than the normal three-hour range.

••••••

"Damn, how the fuck we gon' get outta this muthafucka?" Trey asked as she picked up a chair to smash the kitchen window above the sink because the alarm automatically sealed the doors. Queen was standing in the doorway off the small back hallway. They were so worried about how to get out, they totally forgot about the owner of the house, who was now standing behind Queen with his Glock pressed to the side of her head, demanding Trey and Lilac put down their weapons.

"Come on man, it ain't even gotta be like this. Let's talk this out," Queen said.

"You're in a hell of a position to make any fuckin' requests," Xavier told her, applying pressure to the pistol in his hand. "Now tell your friends to drop the damn weapons."

"Do it," Queen ordered.

Trey fiddled with the idea for a moment, playing with the trigger of the loaded gun while holding eye contact with Xavier. Xavier, being from the streets himself, admired that in her, but this wasn't the time for her to try to prove herself. He aimed the other gun at Lilac and Trey slowly complied and placed her gun down on the table. Lilac soon followed behind with her box cutter.

Xavier toyed with the idea of killing them all for the blatant disrespect of his property. "I can't believe I almost got jacked by some fucking broads!" he chuckled out loud. The approaching sirens calmed him and he returned one gun back to his waist, pushed Queen over to the back door and ordered her to unlock the door for the police. Xavier reached behind her and stopped the alarm from blaring.

Xavier reclaimed his Rolex from Queen's arm and the bags from Trey and Lilac. He glanced down inside. "Damn, my silverware? And which one of you triflin' broads threw my meat on the floor? What was the logic in that? "

The officers rushed inside, grabbing each one of the girls with force. They slapped the iron bracelets on each and began leading them down the hallway through the front door.

Xavier told one of the female officers about the young gorgeous intruder he'd left upstairs in the bedroom. "You think she's still there?" the officer asked, checking out Xavier's backside as he climbed the stairs. *Damn I'd love to tap that,* she thought to herself.

Xavier patted his back pocket, smiling to himself. "Oh yeah, she's still there."

Pebbles was sitting on the bed, now back in her own clothes, twirling her thumbs and scared shitless. She didn't know what was happening to the others downstairs. She didn't know what to expect when the man returned. What Pebbles did know was that he was fine as hell. She'd seen him before, she was sure of it, but she just couldn't place from where. When he first saw her in the closet, he seemed in awe of her. It was something in his eyes. But now she was afraid, awaiting his return.

Xavier entered the room followed by the female officer who pulled Pebbles off the bed and began reading Pebbles her Miranda rights. For a moment, a brief moment, Xavier felt sorry for her. She didn't seem as rough as the others. He looked away as the officer placed Pebbles' hands behind her back and cuffed her. Pebbles eyes pleaded with his the entire time and as the officer led her out of the room. Pebbles mouthed a heartfelt, "I'm sorry," to Xavier. Why did that touch him in a soft way?

He let them out of the front door of the house where they met up with the others, and he watched as the officers led her and the others into awaiting patrol cars.

Trey almost fainted when she saw a tearful Pebbles being led from the home. She quickly shot Queen and Lilac a look that could kill. They had almost left her behind! Trey was pissed at herself more so than at the others because she should have been more reluctant for Pebbles to tag along. She knew this wasn't Pebbles' flavor and now there she was, in the patrol car next to her, crying her eyes out.

"Aey, Pebbles, don't cry. I'll take care of this. I'll call Butta and have her get you out in no time, a'ight? You stronger than that. I taught you better than that. I'll handle this. A'ight? "

Pebbles slowly shook her head. She saw her future flash before her and it wasn't a good one. College! What would happen to college if she went to prison? Could she still pursue her dream of owning a business someday? At that moment, she couldn't see anything past the bulletproof glass directly in front of her.

Chapter Three

Xavier sat on the bed and shook his head, thinking about the attempted burglary. He couldn't help but to chuckle to himself, *Some ghetto bitches actually tried to jack me!*

He lay back on the bed and stretched out his arms. "I can't believe this shit! And the dike-ish one actually thought she was tough!"

The cell phone rang behind him. He reached over and picked up the tiny device, not paying any attention to what he held inside his hand. "Yeah?"

"Hello!" the soft, broken voice said as it came over the phone. "Hello! Is this LaShey's phone? Have you seen her? I'm worried sick about her. It's not like her to be out this late. This is her grandmother, Betty."

Xavier was kind of moved by the elder woman's voice and concern. He didn't want to upset her so late in the night by telling her what her granddaughter and her friends had been up too.

"Ma'am, uhh, LaShey and some other friends were over earlier this evening with my, uhh, with my younger sister. And she must have left her phone here, but I'm sure she's okay. It's nothing for you to worry about. You should get some rest. I'm sure she just fell asleep over one of her friend's house."

Xavier wanted to reassure her that Pebbles was okay. "She's a good, girl you know. LaShey never gives me any problems. You're probably right, I'm sure she'll be home in the morning. Thank you so much, young man."

"You're welcome, ma'am. Have a good night."

Xavier lay back again on the bed thinking of the lovely burglar. How beautiful she was, how she looked in Stephanie's dress, better yet, how she looked *before* she put on that dress. His manhood quickly responded to the thoughts of her and Xavier quickly decided he needed a cold shower.

Xavier straightened up the bed, turned out all the lights and closed the door to he and Stephanie's paradise. *It will never be the same inside that room again,* he thought as he walked down the tan carpeted hallway to the guest room where he'd slept since that fateful night he lost the love of his life.

His cell phone began to vibrate on his waist as he unbuttoned his gray and white Versace shirt, and answered it. "Yeah?"

It was his connect letting him know that the shipment Xavier sent had been received and the wire transfer had been completed to his business account at the liquor store.

He had just made another fifty grand, half his and half the New Yorkers' he blazed with. He removed his belongings from his pants pockets placing them on the black marbled dresser. Pebble's ID was still in his possession. He'd forgotten to give it to the female officer when she came upstairs to get Pebbles. Xavier picked up the license and slowly looked it over. Her birthday revealed her true age, eighteen. She was far to young to be involved in such bullshit.

Eighteen, he thought. She was the same age as Stephanie when they began dating. So young and so sweet.

He stared at the face on the ID. She truly was a beautiful young lady. Something about her stirred him inside, things he felt guilty for feeling. Women often thought of Xavier as being heartless and cold because he showed little emotion or feeling towards them, but Xavier made a promise to Stephanie, a promise he intended to keep.

He threw the ID back onto the dresser and decided to hand it to an officer in the morning when he went down to press charges against the lovely felon and her crew.

As Xavier was stepping out of the shower, Pebbles' phone rang again. Xavier wrapped himself in a towel and returned to the bedroom. He reached to grab the phone, thinking it was her grandmother again, still worried sick. He lay there silent as the voice of the pretty intruder came through the receiver.

"I was wondering if I left my phone there. I was hoping you could drop it off or mail it, along with my ID to the address shown on the ID. I know that's some pretty bold shit to ask of you, especially after we broke into your house and all but..."

"I'll drop it off," he told her, hanging up the phone in her ear.

He lay there, her voice still ringing in his ear. *What the hell is up with this chick? She got balls, I'll give her that.*

He wondered why he wasn't all that upset with the burglary, at least not Pebbles' part. Could it have been because it was him that was once a young intruder, breaking in homes across the city with his friends in high school? But deep inside he knew it was more than that where she was concerned. Why couldn't he stop thinking about her? He grabbed the remote and turned on the stereo he had mounted inside the headboard of his queen-sized bed. He tried to fall asleep to the sounds of the Quiet Storm.

He thought of Stephanie, his love for her and how that love had kept him from letting any other woman get close to him. He'd never brought another female, besides Patricia, Stephanie's mother, inside the home they once shared.

If a woman was an asset to him, Xavier would simply put her in an apartment close by and accessible to him. Xavier demanded privacy and Pebbles had already violated that rule, as well as his space and his mind.

As Rome played over the speakers, "*...Every time I see your face, it makes me wanna sing, and every time I think about your love it drives me crazy...*", He closed his eyes to the thoughts of a beautiful lady--Pebbles.

••••••

Upset at the sudden disconnection, Pebbles returned the phone to its cradle, furious. She had waited over an hour for her one phone call. "He hung up on me!" she said, staring at the girls.

"What the fuck did you expect him to do? You just jacked the muthafucka. Did you honestly expect him to hold a damn conversation with yo' ass?" Lilac laughed.

Pebbles knew he would still be upset but she didn't expect him to hang up in her face. She didn't know why, she just didn't. Truth be told, her feelings were a little hurt.

"Aey, bitch, phone check." The command came from a big burly looking woman, with braids to the back and a long scar running from her left eye to her chin. Pebbles looked up at the giant and then to Trey, who was sitting on the silver metal bench across the holding cell, already sizing her up.

"What, you deaf bitch? I said it's a muthafuckin'..."

Before she could finish the sentence, Trey had lit into her from the left side and Lilac from the right. Blows were coming from everywhere. The mouthy woman's face met the iron bars as Trey kicked her in the abdominal region. Queen got a piece of the action, stomping the huge chick when she hit the ground.

Pebbles stood off to the side, not lifting a finger except to redial her cell phone number. It was turned off. Now, she was really pissed. She slammed down the phone and released a gush of saliva in the girl's now bloodied face.

"Daaammmmnnn! You got knocked the fuck out!" Pebbles teased in her best Chris Tucker voice. "Don't ever try to fade me bitch! I'm with the North side Clit. Next time you disrespect me, expect this ass whoppin' to come back two times strong, smell me? Now yo' fat ass can use the phone."

The guards ignored what was happening inside the cell as they doubled over in laughter. The inmate had been unruly all evening and the CO's were happy to see her get what she'd been asking for…a true ass whippin'.

Trey wiped her hands on the girl's shirt, stepped over her and grabbed the phone. It was the third time that night she had tried to reach Butter. She finally answered on the third ring.

Butter damn near fainted when she saw the phone number on the Caller ID box. "Trey! Trey, baby are you alright? Why you callin' from St. Louis County Jail?"

Trey held her hand up as if Butter could see it. "Aey, Butta baby, you gotta calm down. We a'ight. Shit just got twisted and we got caught up. I need you to get that card outta the box in my drawer and call that attorney. Be here in the morning at nine A.M., ya heard me? Aey, and I need you to do me a favor. If the bail is to steep, I want you to post bond fo' Pebbles first, a'ight?"

Butter couldn't have heard that correctly. *Leave Trey in a jail full of horny women and bond out Pebbles? Not a chance!* Butter wasn't crazy. Jail could be heaven-on-earth to a stud broad like Trey.

"Trey, you don't expect me to leave you in there, I know."

"Look, Butta. I can't have Pebbs in this fuckin' place. Time ain't an issue for me and I ain't new to this. Hell, she ain't never even been sent to the damn principal's office. Besides, Nana will kill my ass. Just do as I say. Lil' East-Bay owe me some grip. Handle Pebbs and go holla at him, then worry about me, a'ight?

Butter didn't respond.

"A'ight? Look, baby, it's gon' be a'ight. Just let me do this."

"A'ight, Trey, its blue, baby. I'll be there in the morning. I love you," Butter replied.

"I love you too, baby, bluer than blue, you feel me?"

Trey heard a quiver in Butters voice.

"Don't start that crying shit. Yo' back too strong fo' that. Just try to get some sleep. Its already one in the morning, you'll see me before you know it, a'ight?"

Butter hung the phone worried sick, despite Trey's heroic attempt to reassure her. Trey was already on probation for possession. This would definitely violate her and she would be looking at major time. Butter wiped her eyes, walked over to the dresser drawer and removed the tiny white box from under Trey's boxers. The fancy writing on the card read, "April Clyne, Attorney at Law."

Ms. Clyne had come through for Trey time after time. She was well respected in the St. Louis area and rubbed noses, among other things, with ninety five percent of the DA's and judges in town. She met Trey and the crew through a mutual friend and began representing them in exchange for *bunk*, a high and potent grade of weed.

Butter placed the call to handle her business. April agreed to meet her at the station in the morning. Butter curled up in the bed underneath the covers praying for yet another miracle for Trey. She wanted so badly for Trey to leave all this bullshit alone. She had too much potential to be running around with those petty ass PMS gangstas.

Butter only joined the crew because it would keep her close to Trey. She desperately loved Trey and would do anything to save her. even if it meant calling her ex-boyfriend.

Jayson was a big time baller who treated Butter like a queen--her and his three other women. Everything was equal amongst them, including them all getting pregnant. Butter chose wisely to have an abortion rather than carry his seed.

Butter had given Jayson all her loyalty and asked no questions until Trey brought the truth to her, forced her to accept it and fucked the shit out of her that very same night. It was magical for Butter. She had never been with a woman lover before, although she had honestly been curious about since she met Trey through Pebbles. Trey had done things to her body that night that she never knew could be done. She experienced the most explosive orgasms she had ever felt. The following morning, Trey accompanied Butter to the abortion clinic, stuck by her side and remained there. For that reason alone, her undying loyalty now lied with Trey and it always would. But sometimes, usually times like this, Butter wondered…

••••••

Lilac called her mother, Shirley, and broke the news to her over the phone. Her mother hung up the phone without a word or a second thought. She'd be right down. She'd sit in the lobby of the county jail until morning need be to get her only child out on bail.

Shirley was vocally disappointed with the way Lilac chose to live her life and her choice of friends, but she loved her unconditionally and right or wrong, continued to stand by her. She knew that God would one day intervene.

Every night, when the gunshots went off, Shirley would hit her knees and asked God to bring Lilac home safely, and every night thus far, God had been faithful to answer. In Shirley's eyes, The Clit was like a drug to Lilac, an addiction that left her so strung out that Lilac constantly needed a fix and there was no place Lilac could go to detox from the crew she had come to love more than life, it seemed.

Shirley pulled herself out of her squeaky brass bed, dressed herself and called an Allen Cab. She contemplated along the ride to St. Louis County Jail how Lilac could have grown to be so violent.

Could it be those horrible fights she witnessed between me and her father all those years? Or could it have been the beatings her father would burn into Lilac's skin as well? Maybe, it was…

Shirley shook her head and sighed. She didn't want to indulge that thought.

So many times Lilac would go to school in summertime temperatures with long sleeves and long legged pants on, hiding the extension cord marks caused by her drunken father, Willis. Whatever the reason was, Shirley was sure her upbringing was at the core of Lilac's defiance and rebellion against both Shirley and the law.

She dried her eyes as the cab pulled up in front of the police station. *Maybe*, she thought to herself, *I keep coming to help her 'cause I didn't have the strength to help her back then. But Lord, you know I wasn't even strong enough to help myself.* She reached for the cross around her neck and said a prayer before paying the driver and heading inside.

••••••

Queen sat there staring at the phone. She had no one to call. Her mother couldn't bail herself out half the shit she got herself into, let alone Queen. She had money stacked at the house but dared not to tell her crack-dependant mother where it was. "Aey, Trey, when you handle yo' business, stop by my crib and handle mines."

"It's blue, homie," Trey said, slapping Queen some dap.

Queen smiled at her.

"You know I got yo' back. Out and back within the hour."

They finally dozed off and waited for morning to arrive and decide their fates...and change their lives forever.

Chapter Four

"**W***hy you wanna act like we don't be making love and you know we be tearin' it up, breaking stuff, that ghetto love…*".

"...Ooooh, daddy, that feels so good! Go deeper, please go deeper!" she moaned. He placed his hands underneath her pelvis and thrust down inside her with all his weight, the tip of his jimmy resting comfortably beneath her womb. He was in heaven. They rolled over placing her on top. She wrapped her ankles beneath his calves, gripped the sheets and took him for the ride of his life.

"Damn, that feels good baby!" he whispered. As she felt him swell inside her, she released the death grip her pussy had on his jimmy and engulfed it into her mouth. Harder and harder she stroked, impatiently waiting for him to fill her with his want.

His grip on her shoulders grew tighter, his breath shortened and he felt his body about to explode. But before he could, the bedroom door swung open and there she stood, gun cocked and aimed directly at his head. "*Stephanie!*"

Xavier jumped from his sleep, wiping his sweat as he reached over to shut off the alarm clock. He'd been dreaming about Pebbles. *What the fuck? I'm really trippin'!*

He set the clock back down on the nightstand and headed for the bathroom. He stood there with his jimmy drawn, releasing his bladder and wondering why he couldn't get this woman out of his head. It was seven-thirty and he had to be at the station at eight-thirty.

He jumped in the shower, groomed and dressed in a black, made-to-fit Armani suit.

Thelma, his maid, greeted him at the bottom of the steps with a cup of Cappuccino. "So glad to see you're alright, *señor*. I heard about last night. Glad to know you weren't harmed."

Xavier eyed her suspiciously as he removed the cup from her hand and walked past her over to the couch. "Sit down, Thelma."

He stretched out his hand and the middle-aged, small-framed woman took a seat across from Xavier and awaited his orders.

"Last night, four intruders entered this house undetected. Do you know how that was possible?"

Thelma looked dumbfounded. "No, *señor*, I do not."

Xavier believed in his heart that she had unintentionally left the house disarmed. She had never shown this kind of incompetence before, but the mere fact that it could've cost him seventy grand plus, meant that he had to let her go.

"Well, Thelma, its because you didn't turn the alarm on when you left yesterday evening."

Thelma looked as if she was retracing her steps from the previous night in her mind.

"For that reason, Thelma, I'll need you to gather your things and leave my home. I'll give you a reference for any future employer, but I cannot have people around me that I can't depend on."

The humble servant realized her mistake, shook her head in agreement and accepted the consequences for her neglectful behavior. She quietly rose from the couch and gathered her belongings and walked out the door without another word.

Xavier was not a man of second chances. Once you crossed him the first time, there was no second opportunity. He gathered Pebbles' photo ID and phone along with his own and headed for the door. He doubled back, checking to make sure his alarm was set before exiting the house.

••••••

Butter arrived at the police station and greeted April within minutes of Xavier's entrance. When April and Xavier made eye contact they smiled at the thought of a previous meeting, one that kept Xavier from going to prison years back.

April had come highly recommended and she proved to be worth every dime spent both in and out of the courtroom. Outside the courtroom, she wined and dined the DA at Xavier's expense, leading to evidence mysteriously disappearing and the charges against him eventually being dropped.

They hadn't seen each other since then, partly because Xavier no longer got his hands dirty in coke sales on the streets, and partly because he'd slept with April at his celebration party later that evening. He felt he'd owed her one night of meaningless sex, if nothing else. Xavier hated mixing business with pleasure so he ended it with April as quickly as it had begun. After all, he reasoned, she made a much better attorney than lover.

"Xavier, baby, how are you? What brings you here to the station? Surely not trouble I hope."

Xavier leaned in and placed a kiss on her cheek, noticing the beautiful girl standing behind her. He stared at the woman for a moment, checking her out from head to toe. "Client?" he asked, nodding his head towards Butter.

"Naw, came to bond out her girlfriend and crew."

"Girlfriend? Please tell me something that beautiful is not gay."

April shook her head.

"Damn, what a waste of good meat!" he commented looking back to April. "Anyway, no, I'm not in trouble. Four small time gang bangers broke into my home last night and tried to straight jack me. Here's the funny part though. They're girls! Can you fucking believe that? Girls! Anyway, I came down here to do all the paperwork and press charges against them, formally."

"Ah, this is too funny," April said, grabbing Xavier's arm. Xavier gave her a scowling look. "No, no, baby, not funny in that way. Funny in the way that that's who I came to represent."

"Really? And how is it that these small time hoodlums can afford your services? It cost me a grip. Shit, they petty!"

April smiled. "Not as petty as you think. Xavier, take a walk with me."

She looked back to Butter, winked at her and turned back to Xavier. "Xavier come on, you know you owe me one. A pretty big one if I remember correctly."

"I know you don't expect me to let these… these plastic ass gangsta's walk away from this! You gotta be crazy, April. They totally disrespected my house, my shit and... and even Stephanie's things. They ain't gettin' away with that. They must be lacin' that shit they givin' you to smoke."

April placed a hand to Xavier's lips. "Look, I came through for you when you needed me most, didn't I? And that wasn't easy. Now come, Xavier, you can spot me this one. From what I hear, they didn't even get anything."

"Uhh, could it be because I came in and interrupted them? Hell, they even had my fuckin' silverware on their way out the damn door!"

"Alright, just gimme something, at least her girl. She's facing major time on a probation violation. Pretend you don't remember seeing her when you're pressing the charges and we're square. All debts paid in full."

Xavier thought about the offer for a minute. He wasn't used to burning bridges, especially one connected to all the major judicial players. And April had come through for him in a major way. He thought and thought and finally he caved in. "A'ight, but on one condition…"

••••••

The broad-shouldered, stocky officer hit the bars with her nightstick, awaking the crew. "LaShey Simpson, you outta here. Let's move."

Trey smiled through half-sleep eyes, knowing Butter had come through once again. Loyalty…she loved that in Butter.

"Tranesha Simpson and Arnelle Williams."

"Lilac."

"Excuse me?" the officer asked.

"Lilac. My name is Lilac. Please don't call me Arnelle. I hate that fucking name," she said flashing her tattoo.

"Whatever, honey. As of right now, your name is Ms. Pre-trial felon and your hearing is going on in about an hour, you and Simpson. Natasha Hudson, we couldn't get you on the docket until after lunch."

Trey rose up and hugged Pebbles. "Tell Butter I said I love her and good looking out."

"Trey, I'll do anything to help her get you outta this, you know that. No matter what it takes."

Trey smiled and nodded. "I know you will, but until then, you gotta hold it down for me. Ride with Butter to holla at Lil' East-Bay in Kinloch to pick up my grip. Don't tell him I'm locked down, just tell him I was tied up with somethin' and I sent you to collect from him. That way that nigga won't try to stunt. And Pebbs, be careful."

"I will."

They embraced and the officer led Pebbles out of the cell after she embraced Queen and Lilac as well.

Pebbles was taken to the property window to sign out and was given back her cash, her jewelry and her shoestrings. She waved at Butter who stood waiting for her out in the lobby. When she looked off to her left, she saw Xavier sitting at the detective's desk, no doubt bringing them all up on formal charges.

He looked so incredibly handsome. His suit made him look twice as good and made his face stand out. Pebbles searched her mind again, wondering where she could have known him from. In the light of the precinct, she was sure she had seen him somewhere before.

She received her property, walked over to hug Butter and deliver Trey's message. "Don't thank me, thank April here. She pulled some strings and got your shit dropped."

Pebbles reached out to shake April's hand.

"Thank you, but how did..."

April held up her hands. "I'll let him fill you in on all the details, and you might not wanna jump for joy just yet," she said, nodding at Xavier.

••••••

When Xavier saw Pebbles talking to April, he immediately excused himself from the detective and rose up from his seat. He walked over to Pebbles and gave her the ID and cell phone he held in his hand. "You really should call home."

Home! Pebbles wondered…

"Umm, maybe you ought to sit down for this one," he told her, directing her to a seat.

Pebbles inhaled the seductive scent of his Curve cologne and almost fainted. She sat in the chair wondering what he had to say to her and why he had dropped the charges against her, not that she wasn't grateful.

"Here's the deal," Xavier began. "What you and yo' home girls did last night was impressive, yet stupid. I should've shot all ya'll ass' for the blatant disrespect of my property. But it took heart and I admire that. Now, I'm not excusing what you did last night, but your grandmother..."

"My grandmother? You called my grandmother!" Pebbles yelled, causing April and Butter to stare.

"First of all, I'ma ask you to calm yo' wanna-be gansta ass down. Second, *you* left the damn cell phone at my house, remember?"

Pebbles dropped her head inside her hands.

"Don't worry," Xavier told her. "I didn't tell her anything. I told her you and your lil' posse were attending a party at my crib with my younger sister and you must've left your phone."

Pebbles looked up at him in grace. Why was he being so nice about all this?

"She was already worried. She didn't need anything like the fact that her granddaughter was out in the dead of night trying to be a damn thief," he exhaled. "It doesn't matter."

Now, you owe me for a new side iron gate, a new lock, and a new safe. Here's the deal, take it or leave it. The only reason you got into my crib undetected was because the maid forgot to set the alarm on her way out. For that, she lost her job. You agree to replace her and all this goes away for you and your cousin, Trey."

"Replace her! As a maid? Your maid? What kind of shit is that?"

"Take it or leave it," he told her.

"I don't know about that. I mean why me?"

Xavier couldn't believe the nerve of this ungrateful little heifer. *Maybe I should've left her ass locked up in the cage with the rest of them.* "Take it or leave it."

"Your wife actually agreed to this?"

"For the last time, take it or fuckin' leave it! You ain't in no fuckin' position to ask no damn questions. Conversation over!"

Xavier stood to leave and gestured for April to come to him.

"I'll take it," Pebbles said, thinking about Trey. "But what about the others?"

"Not my problem--not part of the deal. See you at eight tomorrow morning, on time, no bullshit excuses. I'm sure you remember the way to the house, right?"

"Oh, you got jokes?"

"Plenty," he replied, waving April off. He turned to Pebbles. "Oh, and if you decide not to show up, you'll be Big Bertha's bitch before the sun sets in the west, feel me?"

With that he returned to the desk, spoke with the detective briefly and headed out the station door.

Pebbles couldn't believe what was happening. *Maid? Why would he want me for his maid? That's whack to the fullest.* "Oh well," she said standing. "Beats the shit out of prison!"

Outside the station, Xavier couldn't believe what he'd just done. What was he thinking? This was insane but what was done, was done and he had business with his connect and Sasha to handle. The adventure with the young criminal would have to wait until morning.

••••••

Trey was soon released and ran out to greet Butter and Pebbles. "How the fuck did ya'll pull this shit off?"

April smiled and winked at Trey on her way out the door. Trey made a note to send April something special that evening.

Butter and Pebbles filled Trey in on all the events as they walked outside to the car.

"Maid? Who the fuck that nigga think he is? You ain't nobody's fuckin' maid. Yo' name ain't Kizzie and this ain't the damn plantation. Man, I swear, give a nigga a lil' loot."

"Trey, its cool. If it got us outta there, I'm down for whatever. You'd do the same for me, so kill that," Pebbles said, holding her stomach. "Let's get something to eat, I'm starving!"

"Yeah, me too," Butter chirped in, hugging Trey. "Trey, baby, I'm so glad you're outta there. I missed you so much last night. No business today, okay? I want you all to myself."

"No can do baby. I need to hit Kinloch and Queen's spot and make it back down to the courthouse for her bail hearing. I got thangs to do, but I'll be home tonight, promise."

"Blue?"

"Bluer than blue," Trey responded.

Chapter Five

Xavier left the station and called Sasha. “Morning,” she answered on the first ring, expecting his call. She knew he’d be calling to apologize for not taking her to Atlanta.

“Hey you, what you up to? You still mad at me?”

“How can I stay mad at the man I love with all my heart?”

Xavier quickly dismissed the comment. Sasha was in love with his money, plain and simple, not with him. If being materialistic was a disease, Sasha would be terminal, with no hope of recovery.

“Well anyway, I’m on my way to meet Doug at the store, then I gotta shoot down by the Pawnshop to check on things over there. How about grabbing some lunch?”

“Why don’t I just come over and cook you something?” she asked, hoping for the chance to finally see his home. Once she got inside, she would make it her own, by any means necessary. She’d see to that.

“Don’t go there, Sasha. You already know the deal on that subject. I’ll shoot through and pick you up when I’m done, a’ight?”

Xavier imagined the hand on the hip, neck stuck out pose he was sure she now possessed. “So what? I’m supposed to just sit here all day until you decide to stop by?”

“I’ll make it worth your while, don’t worry.”

Xavier hung up the phone as he pulled into the parking lot of the liquor store he purchased two years before. He exited his 2002 silver metallic Benz, hit the alarm and waved to his neighboring business comrades. He smiled and greeted his cashier, Rosa, as he entered the store.

"Doug made it yet?" he asked.

"He left a package for you on your office desk. Said to tell you he had an pressing engagement but if there was anything wrong for you to call him."

"Thanks, Rosa."

Rosa smiled to herself, *No, thank you, with yo' fine ass!*

Xavier walked into the office, sat down in his black office chair and picked up the brown sealed shoebox. He opened the drawer, retrieved the scissors, cut the tape and lifted the top. It was filled with all the information Doug had collected on one LaShey Simpson, A.K.A. Pebbles.

Xavier flipped through the pages of information containing health records, school records, birth certificate and her mother's arrest and conviction record. *Vivian Simpson. Where do I know that name from?* He couldn't place it but the name rang loudly in his mind. He thought back to Pebbles, how beautiful she was and how he was going to handle being in the same house with him.

He looked at her high school transcripts. She was an A & B student, pretty impressive, set to graduate in a couple months. *What was she thinking?*

He put the papers back inside the box, locked it in the office safe and headed downtown to his meeting after stopping by the pawnshop.

Xavier felt very distinguished among the all white owners of the St. Louis Rams. As he entered the glass walled room, he felt proud to be able to match wits and money with them, even if it was drug money.

"It's a go on the deal, Mr. Winston. All that's needed is your signature," the stocky senior executive said as he offered Xavier a Cuban cigar.

Xavier smiled, took the cigar, placed the contract on top of the smoked glass desk and gave it a once over. He thought of how proud his parents and Stephanie would be of him if they were still alive.

"The deal set up the way I asked?"

"Sure is, fifty percent of all your proceeds will be put into a scholarship fund named after your son to ensure underprivileged children will be able to attend college."

Xavier nodded his head. "Thanks, Bob. I'll have the papers on your desk no later than tomorrow."

They shook hands again and Xavier headed for the door. He should've been celebrating this historic accomplishment but instead, his mood was very solemn. Times like these he missed Stephanie more than life.

As he got into his car, he saw a bluebird fly by his front windshield. It paused as if to smile at him and flew away. "Thanks, Stephanie!"

••••••

Trey dropped Butter and Pebbles at the apartment and headed out to Kinloch to see East-Bay. East-Bay was one of Kinloch's most feared ballers. He was the type of hustler that people deemed heartless. He would kill you over a thirty dollar debt if he felt like stunting that day.

Trey pulled up in front of the one story brownstone home. From the outside of the house, you'd never know a pack of 'hood rats lived inside. The yard was one of the few on the block that actually had grass. Marbled rocks with crystal granite lined the freshly tarred driveway.

"Speak yo' peace," a raspy voice shouted from behind the door guarded by a black iron gate. "It's Trey, homie. Open up."

The locks popped on the door and the Jamaican born gangsta stepped aside to allow Trey entrance. "Whudd up, chief? Have a seat and I'll be back in a sec."

Trey sat back on the blue velvet sofa fluffed with orange pillows. The heavy flow of incense burned her nostrils. *Country ass nigga,* she smirked as she looked at the Rastafarian decorations on the walls.

East-Bay's girl, Ta'Quan, emerged from the bathroom wrapped in a white towel that was so short, Trey could see her bushy lips hanging low like horse nuts between her legs.

She approached Trey and extended her hand to her. "Hey cutie, haven't seen you in a while."

Trey smiled and accepted her hand. "Yeah, it's been a long time. Tae." Trey eyed her up and down. "But I see you still looking good. E-Bay must be knockin' the walls outta that cat, as fat as it is."

Ta'Quan placed one foot on the couch beside Trey and tenderly guided Trey's hand she held between her thighs. It was so hot and wet inside her.

"Tae, I can't do this right now," Trey said, pulling back her fingers. "Not while E-Bay is in the other room."

"Fuck him, Trey!" Ta'Quan said, thrusting her body forward and pushing Trey's hand back inside her. "You know my heart belongs to you. Always has, always will."

The sound of that made Trey dive inside her fiercely with her fingers. Trey had dated Ta'Quan before she and Butter had gotten together. But Ta'Quan was the type of woman you couldn't take home to momma. She was a stripper at the Pink Slip across the river in East St. Louis, with a grave appetite for sex and men. She could never be anything to Trey other than an occasional fuck. Lesbian rule number one: never kid yourself into thinking you can change a bisexual woman into a straight lesbian. Unless you got a platinum tip on your tongue, she'll always want some dick up inside her. Trey knew Ta'Quan still had feelings for her. But Trey felt she had become disloyal to the game when she hooked up with East-Bay, who was supposed to be Trey's partner in the dope game.

Ta'Quan had her nails deep into trey's shirt and grinding her now straddled body across Trey's fingers when East-Bay entered the room.

Trey saw him over Ta'Quan's shoulder and that only made her thrust harder. Trey wanted him to know who Ta'Quan really belonged too. She smiled as Ta'Quan's body shuddered and caved in, landing her head atop Trey's shoulder. Trey kissed her neck and her shoulders before asking East-Bay, "You ready?"

East-Bay bit the inside of his jaw and answered, "It's all here, you can count it if you like," he said, tossing the wad of cash on the couch next to Trey.

Ta'Quan slid to the side of Trey, avoiding direct eye contact with East-Bay. He wanted so badly to kill her skank ass but he knew Trey and the NPG's would come down on him. And they were the last people he wanted to go to war with.

"No need, homie, I trust you," Trey said picking up the purple Crown Royal bag from the seat. Trey made sure the juices on her hand from Ta'Quan brushed against East-Bay's hand when she extended it to him.

She opened the bag and pulled out a small stack of twenty's. "I got a lil' job for you. This nigga named Winston, Xavier Winston, is a future prospect for a business partner. Check him out for me."

Trey tossed the cash at East-Bay, winked at Ta'Quan and walked out the door. Trey smiled to herself because she knew he was about to tear a hole in Ta'Quan's ass, but she smiled even harder at the fact that Ta'Quan didn't care. She cut for Trey enough that anytime, anywhere, any place, it was on...despite the consequences.

••••••

Trey's next stop was Queen's house to pick up her money and head back to the county. Instead, she decided to use her own money to post Queen's bond and reimburse Lilac's mom for Lilac's bond. Trey wasn't looking forward to running into Queen's mother, Rosalyn. Every time they crossed paths, Rosalyn hit her up for money or weed.

When she made it back to the county jail, she found out that Queen's bail hearing had been pushed back and she still had about an hour and a half to kill before Queen's docket was called. Rather than sit and wait, Trey decided to kill some time at the Northwest Plaza Shopping Mall.

Trey's first stop was at the Kay's Jewelers at the entrance of the mall. She wanted to price a promise ring for Butter. She placed the thirty-seven-hundred dollar, two carat diamond cut ring in the layaway with a down payment of twelve-hundred dollars.

She then walked down to Famous Bar and instantly she spotted a very familiar face. It was the owner of the house they'd hit last night. He was in the perfume section sorting through fragrances to purchase.

Trey ducked behind a cargo of boxes stacked in the middle of the floor and watched him. He browsed through the fragrances one by one as if he were an expert in the area. Trey waited until the stranger was out of sight before she continued her shopping journey, picking out some lingerie for Butter and a pair of leather boots for Pebbles.

Trey gathered two leather designer backpacks for their upcoming year of college, equipped with paper, notebooks, pens, calculators, and a wallet. She placed five, one-hundred-dollar bills into each of the wallets and had the bags gift-wrapped.

She proceeded over to the Men's Department to find her some gear to wear to the club later on that night. She figured the crew would be game to go down to Spruils, on Jefferson, and kick after a night like the previous one.

Once she had picked out a pair of black Phem jeans, a matching black and tan stripped Phem shirt and a pair of Phem boots, she headed for the car and made her way down to post bond for Queen.

As she cruised on Highway 270, her phone rang, "*...She's a two-way freak, a two way freak...*". It was her ring tone for Ta'Quan. When Trey answered, Ta'Quan was balling on the opposite end of the phone.

"He hit me, Trey! That rusty muthafucka put his hands on me 'cause of you!"

"'Cause of me? How you figure that?"

"'Cause of what we was doin' on the couch, he said he wasn't gon' keep lettin' me disrespect him like that with you. You know he hate it 'cause I still love you all like that."

"So what you want me to do about that, Tae? You know I can't be out there trippin' and shit in Kinloch with that nigga E-Bay over you. I got a gal, baby, and she ain't gon' have no understandin' of that."

Trey could hear the disappointment in Tae's voice but she had to reserve that level of respect for Butter. Getting into it with East-Bay meant goin' to war. Butter could understand if it was over product or money, but Ta'Quan, she wasn't having it. It's not that Trey didn't care for Ta'Quan and appreciate the loyalty she showed her, but that just wouldn't be a smart move.

"Listen, Tae. I'll talk to him, a'ight? But you can't keep doin' that shit in front that man 'cause you think I'ma be there to protect you all the time, feel me?"

Tae sighed. "I'll handle it, a'ight? Just stop cryin'. I'll get at him later on that, promise."

"I love you, Trey."

"It's good," Trey said and hung up the phone. She couldn't afford to get in the middle of their bullshit but she would holla at East-Bay and let him know that she didn't appreciate the bitch move. To Trey, it was as good as saying "fuck you", and that she would not tolerate, not when she was puttin' food on your table and money in your pocket.

She lit up her blunt and chuckled to herself, *Niggas can be so much like bitches sometimes.*

She inhaled her medication as the words of her favorite rapper laced the track. "*...Ever since I met you, I could peep the pressure. It's like yo' man don't understand, all he does is stress you. I could see the state of misery from the introduction. Can you get away...*".

"Say that shit, Pac!" she yelled as pushed the speedometer to 70 mph.

••••••

As Queen stood before the judge, she was sweating bullets because Trey had not yet arrived for her preliminary hearing. The small-framed white female district attorney arose from her seat and stood at the wooden podium to face the judge. She placed her wire framed glasses down atop the stand and addressed the court.

"The state asks for remand, Your Honor. Ms Hudson is the leader of a ruthless female gang on the city's north side, which is called," she looked down at her note pad. "I believe, the NorthSide Clit. Not to mention, that this is not by far the first run in Ms. Hudson has had with the law. We've also been informed that the defendant is connected to heavy gang activity outside the St. Louis area and may pose to be a flight risk."

"That ain't true!" Queen butted in.

The elderly white man banged his gavel at Queen and spoke as sternly as he could. "Young lady, there will be no more of that in my court room. We don't act like we're in 'the 'hood' when we're in my courtroom. We behave with great dignity and respect. So please, conduct yourself accordingly."

He looked back over to the District Attorney. "Now, the State's request for remand is denied. I'm sure Ms. Hudson doesn't want to deal with me after jumping my bail order, right Ms. Hudson?"

"No sir, I sure don't," Queen answered, finally smiling as she saw Trey enter the courtroom.

"I didn't think so. Bail is set as twenty-thousand dollars. Ten percent cash or property. This court stands adjourned. Next case."

Trey winked at Queen, left the courtroom and went immediately to the court cashier and posted the ten-percent cash for Queen's bond. Two grand was a slap on the wrist.

An hour later, Queen walked out the property room to meet Trey. "Damn, I thought you forgot about me, nigga!" Queen said, hugging Trey.

"Neva that! I told you I had yo' back. I was killin' some time at the mall and you know how I do it. I gets lost up in that muthafucka. Then that bitch, Tae, called me talkin' bout E-Bay done whipped her ass over me."

"Shit, what else is new?" Queen laughed. "You gon' get that trick killed one day."

"Shit, I can't help it if it's like that between us. I mean, I cut for her but at the same time, I ain't finna go to war over her ass."

"Don't I know it, nigga. Good looking out on the money tip too. My momma home when you got there? Please tell me you didn't let her see where my stash was, did you?"

"Naw, I didn't even hit yo' spot. I shot out to Kinloch and got my grip from that nigga, E-Bay. That's why he just dropped them thangs on Tae. She came out the bathroom wearin' nothing but a towel and wanted me to help her get that thang off. Being the nigga I am, I felt obligated."

Queen burst out laughing. "Bitch, you got issues."

"True dat. But anyway, I got my grip and I posted yo' bail outta that."

Queen shook her head. "A'ight, cool. I'll get you back as soon as we hit the 'hood."

"It's good," Trey said. "We need to stop by Lilac's spot on the way. I wanna give Ms. Shirley back her money for Lilac. Then, tonight let's go kick at Spruil's. I need a drink after all that crazy shit."

"You know I'm game, playa."

Once inside the car, Trey filled Queen in on all that had happened with Pebbles and the owner of the house. Queen smiled and hit Trey on the arm.

"Damn, that shit is sweet! Aey, shit that might work to our advantage, nigga. With Pebbs inside, we can gain all the info we need to clean his ass out completely and do the shit right this time," Queen said, smiling to herself.

Trey quickly frowned at the idea of Queen thinking she could use Pebbles like that. "Naw, Q, let that shit go. If you hadn't been lookin' for diamond treasures last night, we could've been outta there before his mark ass came home in the first place. I refuse to put Pebbs in any mo' shit. Did you see the look on her face last night? She was scared shit-less. She couldn't handle that shit, and I'm sorry, dawg, but you nor anybody else is gon' put her in that position again. You can cancel that."

"Damn, nigga, it's just an idea. Why you always bitchin' up over Pebbles and shit?"

"Never mind all that. Come up with somethin' else, Q."

"A'ight, a'ight, calm yo' ass down. It was just a thought. I'll come up with somethin' else," Queen lied. In her head, she was already thinking of how she was gonna make this situation work to her benefit, no matter what it cost or who it hurt.

Chapter Six

"So, what are you gonna do, Pebbles? I mean how are you gonna be around him all day, everyday, as fine as that nigga is and simply keep it strictly business?" Butter questioned as she sipped on her glass of Boone's Apple Blossom Wine.

"Well first of all, *he* made the proposition, not *me,* so he's gonna have to live with it. Secondly, that's all this is, business. Nothing more, nothing less, so I ain't worried about that. Besides, I've been around fine ass men before. Hell, there's plenty of fine ass niggas in the 'hood."

"Yeah, but not *filthy-rich* ass fine niggas," Butter teased.

Honestly, Pebbles had no idea how she was gonna handle being Xavier's maid. She barely cleaned up at home. Her Nana did majority of the housework and even washed her clothes for her. Her mother was never home enough when Pebbles was younger to teach her basic cooking and cleaning skills. Hell, she didn't even know how to iron but she'd soon have to learn. *Shit, how hard could it be?* she wondered.

As for the attraction, Pebbles was sure she could keep her cool. He was attractive, she had to admit, and she sensed it was a two-way street. She could feel him practically undressing her earlier at the police station.

"If he thinks this is a plot to get some, he got me bumped," Pebbles snapped.

"Girl, please! Yo' thong will be down at yo' ankles as soon as you hit the damn door tomorrow," Butter laughed.

••••••

Trey stepped from out of the bathroom dressed to kill. She walked over to the tan dresser and picked up her Eternity cologne and sprayed it across her chest.

"Yeah well, that nigga betta not try nothin' slick, I know that. 'Cause I will lay that nigga down!"

Butter and Pebbles looked at each other and smiled. Trey loved Trey's thuggish nature but Pebbles figured she'd better change the conversation before Trey got too hyped over the situation.

"Damn, Trey! That's a tight ass outfit. What exactly does Phem stand for? Is that some of Phat Pharm's new shit?"

"Naw, Phat Pharm is out of there. This is that new gangsta shit," Trey responded, pointing at her chest. "This shit right hurr, this stands for 'Player Haters Envy Me'. So true, so true. Blue, ain't it?"

"Hell yeah, that shit is tight!" Pebbles agreed.

"An' don't my baby look so damn good rockin' that shit?" Butter said, walking up behind Trey. She wrapped her arms around Trey's waist and placed a kiss on the back of her neck.

"Umm, if you keep doin' that shit, we'll never see the club," Trey said, turning to face Butter. They kissed a passionate kiss as Pebbles slapped her forehead and frowned.

"Aww, here ya'll go with this shit!"

"Don't hate," Butter said as they laughed.

A knock came at the door. Pebbles walked to the living room and opened the front door to allow Queen and Lilac entrance into the apartment.

"What's up, Florence? Where's George and Weezy?" Queen teased.

"Very funny," Pebbles replied with a frown.

"I'm just fuckin' with you. It's all good."

"Ya'll ready?" Pebbles called out to Trey and Butter.

"Hell yeah! Let's be out. I'm ready to get my dance on," Trey said, grabbing her keys off the kitchen counter.

••••••

The club was packed as usual and the crew made their way to the back of the building past the dance floor.

Queen ordered everyone a round of drinks as she stared at a familiar face through the crowd. She nudged Trey on her arm, who was in a trance watching Butter in a mid-thigh high silver spandex dress and silver stilettos, returning from the rest room.

"Aey, aey, Trey. Ain't that that bitch, Carla, that ganked you out that product?"

"Where," Trey asked, rising from her seat.

"Right there, the bitch with the patch of white weave in the front of her hair."

Trey focused in on the middle-aged, light skinned woman. “Yeah, that’s that trick. I oughta go over there and beat that hoe like she stole somethin’.”

“Shit, you know I’m down to get my thug-thizel on! I got hella stress to relieve after last night,” Queen said.

“Trey? Trey, baby, what’s wrong?” Butter questioned, noticing the expression on her woman’s face.

“That’s the skank I told you about. Carla, the one that gave me all them counterfeit twenty-dollar bills for that pound of weed. I can’t believe she got the balls to show her face off up in here.”

“Let’s cancel that bitch nigga, I’m tellin’ you. That’s how you maintain yo’ respect in the ‘hood. If you give her a pass, every weed head on the block will try you.”

Butter pulled Trey closer to her. “Trey, no. We came to enjoy ourselves. Fuck that stupid shit. Can we have just one night where this crazy mess don’t go down?”

“Butter, I know you ain’t ‘hood for real, but if Trey don’t step to that bitch, it’s gutta’ fo’ her in the ‘hood from this point on. It’s all about maintaining the game and yo’ respect at the same time.”

“Fuck the game!” Butter blurted out. They all turned to and stared at her but Butter held her ground.

“Ya’ll asses is lucky to even be sittin’ here right now ‘cause of the *game.* You just spent two grand on bond this morning, Queen. Lilac, yo’ momma works hard fo’ the money she keeps having to spend to get yo’ ass outta trouble.”

Butter turned to Trey. “And baby, yo’ lil’ cousin is about to clean a nigga’s toilet to keep you free. All I wanna know is, what the fuck is the game givin’ you in return?”

“Fuck you mean?” Queen said, standing up.

“Chill!” Trey ordered. She turned to Butter. “Come on, let’s dance.”

Butter enclosed her hand inside of Trey’s as Trey led her to the dance floor.

She grabbed Butter and held her close to her. As the sounds of Jon B filled the club, Trey explained to Butter the issue of respect.

“Butta, baby, you can’t just say shit like that to people. Don’t get me wrong, I love you for the way you speak yo’ mind and don’t take no shit from anybody, but there is a time and a place fo’ everything. You know them hoes is all hotheads. Certain boundaries you can’t cross in the ‘hood. You wanna be with a ‘hood nigga? Then you gotta learn how to be a ‘hood nigga’s girl. You gotta understand that respect is everythang in this world, not just in the ‘hood. If you don’t demand the respect from yo’ peers, people think they can try you. And if you to allow them to succeed you might as well become a doormat for everything and everybody, feel me?”

Butter lay her head on Trey’s shoulder. “Yeah baby, I feel you.”

“*...Don’t listen to what people say, they don’t know about, bout you and me. Put it out yo’ mind ‘cause it’s jealousy, they don’t know about this here...*”.

Queen sucked her teeth at the sight of Butter and Trey. "That bitch is makin' Trey soft with all that county ass mentality. Follow me Lilac."

"Where ya'll going?" Pebbles asked.

"To handle that bitch," Queen spit out.

Pebbles stared as the girls made their way through the crowd. She wanted to join in on the altercation but she knew Trey would be livid so she stood up in her chair and awaited the festivities.

The small-framed female was sitting at the bar downing a Margarita as the first blow struck her face from the left side, hard enough to knock her off the bar stool and onto the floor.

Queen stood above her and demanded for her to get up. The woman looked up at Queen and quickly became frightened as she focused in on the familiar face.

"Yeah bitch, remember us? You thought you could gank my home girl and get away with it? Now it's time to pay the piper," Lilac said, pulling the woman up by her hair.

The woman tried to fight back but against the combination of Lilac's fist and Queen's elbows, she didn't stand a chance.

Trey released Butter as she watched the security guards rush over towards Queen and Lilac. "Shit, these bitches is straight trippin. Aey, baby, go on over to the table and stay there with Pebbles, you hear me? No matter what go down, don't leave that table until I call you on your cell phone, a'ight?"

Butter frowned and shook her head. "I'm so tired of this shit, Trey."

She turned to walk away as Trey made her way through the crowd to help her crew. Right or wrong, she vowed to have their back.

Security consisted of two big husky men dressed all in black. Trey reached the scene as the guards grabbed a hold of Queen and Lilac.

"Get off me!" Lilac shouted, kicking and screaming. "Let me go!"

"Get yo' fuckin' hands off me!" Queen demanded to the bigger guard.

"Clam ya'll asses down!" the smaller guard yelled. "Ya'll gotta get the hell outta here. Ya'll do this shit every time ya'll come up in here."

Trey looked down at the lumped up woman on the floor trying to gather her composure. Sitting on the bar above her was her purse. Trey reached behind the guard, grabbed her purse, cuffed it underneath her arm and then followed the guards as they pushed Queen and Lilac toward the front entrance.

Trey was furious at Queen and Lilac for taking matters into their own hands. If she wanted to confront the lil' clucker, she would have done it herself. She didn't want their help nor need their help. She was far from being a punk.

"Fuck is wrong with ya'll?" Trey asked them once they all got outside of the club.

"Fuck you mean, Trey? We handled that bitch for you," Lilac argued.

"Butter's right, ya'll. We don't need no heat right now. Did ya'll forget ya'll on bail right now? I was gon' handle that bitch on the low. I just didn't wanna do in front of Butter. Damn man! Ya'll trippin," Trey said, dialing Butter's cell phone to tell her grab Pebbles and come outside.

Queen and Lilac looked at Trey in disbelief. "The fuck is up with her?" Queen asked Lilac.

"*Like Butter baby, finger lickin' good,*" Lilac said, mimicking Trey.

Queen smirked. "Fuck them hoes."

"Yeah well, I bet that lickin' ain't as good as the one you put across that bitch's head. You hit that hoe with a straight whammy," Lilac said, laughing as her and Queen walked back towards her Impala to wait for the rest of the crew.

••••••

Pebbles sat up in her bed, mind swirling about the next morning. It was Saturday and she wasn't happy about spending it cleaning some rich man's mansion. Not just any man, a fine, young, African American *tenderoni.* She got out of the bed, walked over to the bathroom and looked herself over. Her hair was still a mess from spending the night in jail and the humidity of the club didn't make it any better. Her nails looked unmanicured and she definitely could use a facial.

She pulled the apricot scrub from the cabinet, went into the bedroom and turned on her favorite Lyfe Jennings CD. It would be a long night.

She removed her nail kit from the broken mahogany dresser drawer and began a late night "diva shock treatment." As the sounds of Life massaged her soul musically, she applied the facial scrub to her face, followed by an olive oil based hot oil treatment to her hair.

"*...Must be nice, having someone who loves you despite what they've heard. Someone who mighty as a lion but still as gentle as a blue bird. Must be nice, having someone who understands that a thug has feeling too...*".

Four hours later, at three-forty A.M., she was done and she was beautiful, her face flawless, her nails softly colored and sophisticated, and her hair, roller wrapped and ready.

"Why am I doing all of this? He's married, right?" she asked herself, crawling back between the purple and magenta colored covers. "It's not like he's my man or nothing."

She lay there trying to calm the anxiety that was keeping her awake. She had to be at his front door in less than five hours and the last thing she needed was bags underneath her eyes.

••••••

Trey had dropped Butter off after the club scene and made a run with Queen and Lilac. The keys jingled in the lock and Butter's heart fluttered. Her baby was home! Butter had already planned out her moves. She knew what Trey like best and Butter felt that if she had to use her body to heighten her influence over Trey, she had no problem doing just that.

After her shower, she rubbed her body down with Trey's favorite Ralph Lauren fragrance, Blue. She brushed her hair until it lay with heightened sexuality over her shoulders and down her back. She put on a black crotch-high teddy, lay down in the bed and positioned herself in a way that made sure it would expose all her glory to Trey as she entered the room. She then tried to pretend she was asleep.

Trey loved to wake her up and make love to her while Butter was lying on her stomach. With her legs bucked open wide, she was sure Trey would dive right in. She was right!

The sight of her openness made Trey's knees buckle. The music was playing, the scented candles were burning and her woman had fallen asleep while waiting up for her. She wouldn't disappoint her.

Trey set down the gifts she'd brought for her and Pebbles, softly crept into the bathroom, showered and came back into the room with the water still dripping from her body. *No time to dry off and lotion up,* she thought to herself. *It's been a long ass day--too long!*

She opened the white chest, pulled back her stack of shorts and grabbed what she came for. It's life-like feel and seven-inch size drove Butter crazy on every occasion. Trey strapped it on, lubed it up with KY Jelly and softly climbed onto the bed. She didn't want to wake her beforehand, wanting to fuck her while she was asleep so she'd think she was dreaming. It is a known fact that women get twice as wet when fantasizing in their sleep.

Trey towered over Butter's backside and admired the plump cheeks underneath her. Then she slid in, uninvited yet always welcomed. The moans of approval came sweetly and quickly.

"Oh, Trey!"

It was the ultimate ego booster. Wanna know if your woman is cheating on you with someone else? Slip inside her in the middle of the night, guaranteed, you'll find out.

"Yeah baby, I'm home."

She placed a series of soft kisses onto Butter's neck and cheek.

"Grind for me."

Butter, fully awake (never really asleep), arched her back and began to gyrate her hips against Trey's pelvis. Trey loved to watch her move. She moaned and screamed as Trey stroked harder and harder. When Butter was about to reach her peak, Trey pulled out and flipped her onto her back. She never cared for a toy to reap the rewards of her hard work.

Butter opened wide to allow Trey to taste her. Trey stuck her tongue inside and beat Butter's clit until she let a flow of juices out into her mouth. Butter's body quivered and her voice cooed. She gripped Trey's head for dear life. When she calmed down and was able to speak, she whispered, "Give me what I want."

Butter, flipped back onto her stomach. The sweat puddling in the crease of her back turned Trey on even more. She spread Butter's cheeks apart and placed her own clit directly underneath the tailbone between them. As Butter grinded and contracted the muscles in her butt cheeks, she pulled Trey's clit and massaged it until it swelled and Trey collapsed on top of her both exhausted and satisfied.

"Damn, I love you girl!" Trey sputtered out, breath far and between.

Butter turned over, grabbed Trey by the cheeks and asked, "Blue?"

"Bluer than blue," Trey responded. Trey slid the flesh like stallion back inside Butter and began on another journey into a world where stereotypes and discrimination of their lifestyle didn't exist--a place were both gay and straight alike felt heaven.

••••••

Sasha sprayed the Corvontiere perfume on her strapless shoulders for the third time since Xavier had given it to her earlier that day. She'd hoped it would entice him to do a little something.

No can do. His mind was preoccupied with the next morning and the newly hired cleaning lady. None of the things he had swimming through his mind made sense concerning her, like why he'd offered her a job in the first place.

"Xav, why are you so gone tonight?" Sasha asked as she slid her hands down into his Sean Jean black slacks.

"Long meeting," he answered, not really wanting to lie, but knowing that she didn't really care for real. If it didn't drastically affect his incoming dollars, she could care less.

He was semi-hard for what seemed like hours, despite the fact that his jimmy was engulfed into Sasha's mouth. He closed his eyes and imagined for a moment. Imagined a different ending to the night before. Imagined himself sliding his hands up her thighs when he walked over and bent down to retrieve her ID. Imagined the sound it made when his fingers entered inside and plunged deeply between her lips. Imagined the feel of her breath upon his neck as he lay her down upon one of the floor-length mink coats in the closet and entered her with all of him. Imagined the moves, the moans, the heat, the wetness...the...the...cum he'd just squirted out.

Sasha looked as if she'd die right there on the spot. With globs of sperm hanging from her chin, she stormed off to the bathroom screaming, "How could you? Uhh, it's disgusting!"

Xavier chuckled to himself and was more than happy to oblige her request when she told him to get the hell out and go home.

Chapter Seven

D*ing-dong! Ding-dong!* Xavier rolled over and looked at the clock. "Shit!" he said, hopping out the bed and flinging a towel around his waist. "Eight-o-five. How the hell did I oversleep?"

Then he realized he'd fired the person responsible for setting his alarm clock according to his posted schedule. "Dammit!"

He jogged down the steps, cut the alarm and swung the door open. She was a breathtaking sight, a beautiful sight to see to start the day. "I see you found the place."

"I see you still think you Chris Tucker with the jokes."

He laughed, closed the door behind her and turned to find her staring at him wide-eyed as he stood before her in nothing but a towel. "Oh, I overslept. Maria use to set the alarm for me."

"Maria, is that your wife?"

"Nope, the maid. Anyway, I need to go freshen up. In the meantime, get acquainted with the layout of the house. You know that which you already don't know, being you just tried to clean me out two nights ago," he yelled as he climbed the stairs to shower.

Pebbles rolled her eyes. "Fuck you," she whispered. She hadn't seen the downstairs of the house the other day past the kitchen and the entrance hallway in which she now stood. She walked into the living room, placed her things on the tan leather sofa and began to take in the painting and portraits. Her eyes focused on three portraits. One of a handsome couple she assumed were his parents because the gentlemen and Xavier bore the same nose and bedroom eyes.

The second, one smaller than the other two, was a picture of a Naomi Campbell reject. "Must be his wife. What the hell he see in her," she mumbled.

The third, was a portrait of a young beautiful woman lying across Xavier's lap in front of the fireplace. She was important to him. She could tell by the way their bodies touched and seemed to melt together. "No, that's definitely wifey."

She walk down the hallway, found her way to the kitchen and began to search the beautiful cabinets for the coffee grounds to make her new boss and his wife a pot of fresh coffee. She assumed she'd finally meet the misses. *I wonder did he tell her the truth about me?*

She continued searching the cupboards thinking, *Now I know there's some in here somewhere, all rich people drink coffee. At least they do on TV.*

She spotted the gold and black container, grabbed the Folgers and made her way to the navy blue coffeepot on the counter. She scooped the coffee into the filter free compartment and filled the back tube with water and turned it on. As the ground black coffee made its way from the spout to the pot, Pebbles smiled. *Piece of cake!*

She walked over to the refrigerator and frowned upon viewing its contents. *No bacon! No Sausage! No eggs! Damn, don't these people shop?* "Okay, so what am I supposed to make for breakfast?"

She saw a London and Sons bag on the shelf and removed it. It contained a half-eaten chicken wing dinner. She popped it into the microwave, the one appliance she could use, stood and watched it for a few minutes and then placed it on a plate.

She then made a cup of coffee and placed it, along with the plate of wings, over at the counter where Xavier was now seated in a pair of Fubu jeans and a T-shirt.

Xavier looked down at the plate. "Uh, chicken for breakfast?"

"That's what I saw, there's no bacon or sau..."

"I don't eat pork. Milk and sugar for my coffee, please." He turned on the 13 inch TV at the end of the counter. He frowned at the segment of news, as President Bush pussyfooted around the subject of the weapons of mass destruction Iraq supposedly owned.

"You follow the war?" Xavier asked.

"What for? We got enough wars going on right here at home to be worried about them people."

Xavier raised a curious eyebrow and said, "You don't think they're connected?"

Pebbles brushed her hair from her face and hunched her shoulders. "Do you?" she asked in return.

Xavier chuckled because that would've been the exact same answer he'd gotten from Stephanie.

Xavier fixed his coffee and held it to his lips to sip. Out came a mountain of coffee grounds into his mouth. "What the! Did you use a filter?"

"A what?"

She looked genuinely confused. "Oh, Lord, what have I done?" was all he could muster up as he rose from the stool, headed down the hallway, picked up his keys and cell phone and headed for the door.

"Will your wife be down for breakfast?"

"Naw, you eat it and enjoy. The supply closet is right off the kitchen. All you gotta do is clean. Top to bottom. My cell number is on the desk by the phone. Don't call me unless it's an emergency. I'll be back shortly. You are to stay here until I get back."

He turned to leave but not before giving Pebbles one last piece of advice.

"Oh, and LaShey, if you're thinking about letting your cousin over again or getting sticky fingers again, please don't fuck with me."

With that, he left. Pebbles flipped him the bird while mimicking his John Gotti attitude: "*Don't fuck with me!*"

She sighed as she thought of all the chores that awaited her. This was a huge house. His wife...where was she? *Oh well*, Pebbles said to herself and headed for the supply closet.

"Damn! It's a lot of shit up in here. Which one am I suppose to use?"

••••••

"Damn, coffee without a filter and chicken wings for breakfast," Pedro laughed. "Damn, homes! You better trade her ass in quick."

"Naw, can't do that. She owes me and she got work to do."

Pedro shook his head. "You one strange dude, *papi*."

"You should've seen 'em, Pedro. They really thought they were gangtas. All except this one. She was out of place, out of her league."

"Yeah, but makin' her yo' maid, what's the sense in that?"

"I wish I had answer for that, Pedro, I really do."

They sat in the parking lot awaiting their connection for what was to be Xavier's final drug transaction. The deal was now sealed with the other owners of the Rams, and Xavier could now wash his hands clean of drug money.

Pedro had called down the Brooklyn boss to personally see the deal through and extend well wishes to Xavier from the Brooklyn family. Pedro was one of the few drug dealers Xavier trusted with his money and product. It had become more like a brotherhood over the last seven years they had dealt with other. Pedro had proven his loyalty to Xavier time and again, willing to lay down his life for his friend at the drop of a dime.

Xavier had tried to talk Pedro into investing with him in the upcoming football venture, trying to get him to leave this life alone and roll with him, legit style. But Pedro had his mind made up. He would inherit Xavier's street business and attempt to rule the city.

"You need to seriously think about giving this up, man," he bargained with Pedro. "This shit is getting hectic out here with this meth and shit making waves. It's getting crazy."

"No need to worry about me, my friend. I got it all under con..."

No sound was made except the thump of Pedro's cranium, half-blown apart and hitting the steering wheel. Glass flew across his limp body into Xavier's face as the young Brooklyn gunners took aim at him from every angle.

No, this ain't happening in broad fuckin' day light!

He looked at the hit men, accessing how deep they were. He reached for his nine from under the seat and instinctively took his left hand and removed Pedro's gun from his front waist.

If it's going down like this, I'm goin' out like a soldier.

As Xavier searched his mind for his next move, out of the back of SUV appeared the Brooklyn boss, dressed to kill in a black Gucci suit, black gaiters and dark Gucci shades. The young assassin looked more like a Wall Street playa than a drug boss. He raised his hands and signaled up in a surrender motion to Xavier as he approached the car. He leaned down and tapped on the window despite the fact that Xavier had two nickel-plated nines pointing at him.

"Come on Xav, put the iron down and let's talk a minute, son. You have my word, no mo' rounds is goin' off, word is bond. Lower the heat and let down the window."

Xavier lay down the left Glock, reached over his lap to the window and hit the descending button. He kept the right Glock pointed and cocked. As he'd said before, the only business partner he trusted was now staring at him with blood oozing from his head and mouth, dead. Xavier's trigger finger became itchy as he looked over to his boy.

"What's all this, man? What the fuck you thinking? We beefin' and I don't know about it? Or is this some kinda message you tryin' to send 'cause I want out?"

"Look, Xav, that had nothing to do with you, so don't take it personal. In this business, you gotta learn to take the bitter with the sweet. Yo' boy was skimmin' off the top of my cut, so he had to be dealt with."

"P? Man, no way!" Xavier said, trigger finger getting antsy. "He ain't even cut like that. This been my man for seven plus."

"Think what you want son, but word is bond. My change has been short for months. That habit he been feedin' has been at my expense, but no more. I came here for two purposes," he said, nodding towards Pedro. "One is done. Shall we continue our business for the day? Afterwards you can clean up and call the pigs."

The Brooklyn boss stood back and snapped to one of his young gunners who went to the SUV to retrieve a black satchel and brought it over to Xavier. "Pop the trunk, son."

Hesitantly, Xavier removed the keys from the ignition and handed them to the young gunman. He was getting more nervous by the minute, noticing a crowd beginning to gather around the area. He kept his finger on the trigger and watched as the young man circled to the back of the trunk. Xavier stayed focused on his connect's body language and eye movement. If this was a jack move, it wasn't gonna be as easy as they'd planned.

Once the briefcase was retrieved, he closed the trunk, walked up, tossed the keys to Xavier and loaded the SUV. His connect extended his hand. "Nothin' personal, son, just business. Good luck! Your business will surely be missed."

The Brooklyn boss turned to walk away. "Oh, and Xav, take off all that bling and shit and get rid of the car along with what's in your hand before you call the cops. 'Cause, if I end up Fed, you end up dead, feel me?"

Xavier gave a slight nod of his head and watched the SUV take off and swerve out of the parking lot. Once the coast was clear, Xavier exited the car, brushed past the crowd on the parking lot and headed inside his store to call the police.

He unlocked the back door to the store and placed his guns, his jewelry, money and dope inside the satchel and locked them inside the ice cooler on the side of the liquor store before the police arrived. His story was simple. He and Pedro were sitting outside the liquor store having a friendly conversation, when they were jacked by a couple of hooded roughnecks. Pedro had refused to give up his things and it had cost him his life.

The police bought the story without compromise. After all, this was St. Louis. Shit like that happened all the time.

Xavier sat perplexed in his office as the coroner removed Pedro's body and the police cleared the crime scene. Pedro's car was towed and Xavier was told he would have to close down the store until the forensic team had completed their work. He sent a visibly shaken Rosa home early.

He sat in his office and thought over his time with Pedro. His friendship, his devotion, his...*habit? Why didn't I see it?* Yes, there were times when Pedro seemed a little overly anxious and spaced out but Xavier would've never believed he had a habit.

He had no wife and kids. Xavier regretted that for him, yet at the same time, Xavier wouldn't have wanted anyone to feel the pain he felt over losing Stephanie. His heart felt heavy just thinking about it.

He cruised to his office bar for his favorite soothing drink. As he put the glass to his lips he remembered his package stashed out in the cooler. He unlocked the back door and peaked out, looked east to west down Page Blvd. and made his way around the front to make sure his law enforcement guests had gone. They had diminished enough for him to sneak around to the side of the building and sneak back inside.

He opened the satchel and placed all his jewelry into the wall safe he had hidden in his office. He stared down at Pedro's chain and cross and frowned. *Cross didn't help you much today huh, bro? Just like Stephanie.*

He placed Pedro's things into the safe, took his wallet, cut it up, along with his ID and all the papers inside. He stared down at the blocks of cocaine and thought of how much it had cost him--the lives of those he loved most in life. It had been because of bricks such as those that he was on a "business trip" out of town the night Stephanie went into labor. Now, it had cost him his friend.

He rose up from the chair and grabbed the pile of cut up papers and headed for the restroom. He flushed the tiny pieces of paper down the toilet. He returned to the office and lifted one of the powdered bricks. He picked up the phone and called his cousin, Slugo, a small time hustler.

"Cuszo, I've got a present for you. You just came up."

Xavier hung up the phone and grabbed the satchel. He would deliver the bricks to his cousin and let him have them for what he paid for them, nothing more. *That's for you, Steph.* He'd had enough…he was out!

••••••

Queen sat down on the orange and brown checkered sofa as she watched her favorite DVD, *Friday*. She was kicked back, smoking a blunt and trying to figure out how she could use Pebbles' situation to her advantage. She needed her charges dropped and she couldn't understand how Pebbles and Trey had succeeded in getting off the hook. Queen knew she was facing major time with this one. She had been in trouble with the law too many times before and even though it was all petty stuff, it tended to all up eventually. This incident for Queen definitely was not probation weight.

She needed a strategy, one that would ensure Pebbles' cooperation and Xavier's recanting of his story. Queen knew Pebbles was book smart, true, but street smart she was not. Queen also knew that with the right persuasion, she could get Pebbles to do as she wanted. In her heart, she knew Pebbles wouldn't choose no punk ass job over The Clit.

As she lit up another blunt, her mother, Rosalyn, walked in the house, looking as if the cat had not only dragged her in, but beat her ass beforehand. Rosalyn stood about 5'4" and once upon a time, possessed a curvaceous frame that now looked as if she was anorexic. Her long, silky black hair now looked as if birds had formed a nest inside it. Her face was painted in street style war paint, smeared over her once beautiful cocoa butter skin. Her red, strapless dress was hanging off one shoulder and looking as if it had never seen the iron. Yes, she'd been at the lounge all night and from the looks of it the broke down pimp trailed behind her through the front door was as well.

"What you doin' here? Ain't you got no job yet? Ya ass don't do nothin' else. You don't work, you don't go to school and you damn sure don't do shit around here. Hell, you ain't shit just like yo' daddy. Must be in the gene pool. He wasn't shit and you makin' a good run right behind him. I'm goin' in the back. Don't bother me either."

"Fuck you!" Queen whispered to herself. "You ain't lookin' much better right now."

Rosalyn returned moments later to a look of disgust on Queen's face. "You probably don't even know him," Queen said. She shook her head and inhaled the intoxicating smoke that helped her forget where she was from, where she lived and most of all, whose child she was.

"Don't worry about who I do or don't know. You don't pay no damn bills round here. Now gimme a sac of weed for me and my company. I know you got some, so hand it here."

"Gimme? Damn, he can't afford to buy you a dime bag of weed? I hope you ain't expecting his cheap ass to pay you for your coochie then," Queen snapped.

Rosalyn stood back and placed her hand on what use to be her hip. "Don't worry about what I do in my own damn house and who pay me what for anything I choose to give up. I'm a grown ass woman. Now shut yo' damn mouth and gimme the damn weed!"

Queen reached into her front jean pocket and pulled out a sandwich bag containing the small dime and dub sacs of the herbs Rosalyn wanted. She reached inside, grabbed the smallest one she could see and threw it on the table. She stood up from the couch and headed for her room. "This shit is sickening."

"Yeah, well move yo' ass out! I'm grown, dammit! You hear me? I'm grown!"

Queen plopped down on her twin-sized squeaky bed and the tears started to stream down her face. She remembered the brief happy years when Rosalyn not only acted like she was grown, but acted like a mother. She used to be so vibrant and full of energy. She used to be an active part of their education and their lives. All that changed when she started allowing the neighborhood 'hood rats to get close to her and hang around the house. She started partying every weekend, smoking joints and staying out for days at a time.

"I hate this fuckin' place!" she mumbled as she squeezed her pillow underneath her face. She wanted to kill every man who used her mother as a punching bag or a sex toy…every man that violated her and treated her like a piece of trash on the street. Queen understood that Rosalyn was partly to blame as well, but Rosalyn was vulnerable and weak--wasn't built for street life.

Rosalyn needed help, serious rehabilitation that welfare was not going to provide. That took money and that nickel and dime shit wasn't gonna cut it. Serving time definitely wouldn't cut it. Rosalyn probably wouldn't make it a year out there alone. Queen could think of so many horrible things Rosalyn would encounter in the streets alone. At least now Queen was there to protect her. She was constantly pulling guns on drunken men who chose to violate her mother physically. One, she even unloaded on before while trying to defend what little honor and self-respect Rosalyn had left.

No, she couldn't leave Rosalyn in the 'hood alone. It was not an option. Which meant she needed those charges dropped, meaning she had to get to work. She picked up the phone and called Lilac.

••••••

Butter beamed as she opened the gifts Trey had gotten for her the day before. "Oh, Trey, I love 'em, I love 'em all! You are so sweet. Here you are just getting out of jail and you're shopping for me."

Trey kissed her on the lips and spoke softly, "You know its all about you, baby."

Butter loved the way Trey spoiled her. Yet she had a desire deep inside for Trey to leave all that "'hood" shit alone. She was growing tired of nights like last night where she had to wait up and pray Trey made it in safely.

Trey pushed Butter constantly toward going to college and Butter wished Trey would follow suit and come along too. She was so intelligent yet she chose the ghetto life over something better. Butter couldn't understand it and she often wondered if maybe Trey was afraid to succeed outside the "Lou", afraid that if she did, it would mean she wasn't really built for "ghetto life."

"Well, baby," Butter began, grabbing Trey around the arm. "School will be starting in a few months. I'll be gon' off to SEMO and I will hardly get to see you. Of course, we can fix all that if you just go with me, and that way we'll still be able to be close to each other all the time."

Trey shook her head and turned away to glance outside the window of their fourth floor apartment. "You know I can't do that."

"You can't or you won't? I don't understand you, Trey. As smart as you are, why don't you wanna go to college?"

"Cause I'm tryin' to get this money to put you and Pebbles through college. Plus, you know I'm tryin' to get this barbershop thing off the ground."

"And you don't think a Business Degree will help you accomplish that?"

"Butta, I don't need no textbook to tell me how to add and subtract my money. The dope game taught me well."

Butter came and wrapped her arms around Trey's waist and lay her head against her shoulder. "Trey, we can get an apartment, we can get some grants and what the grants don't cover, we can take out in loans."

"No!"

"But Trey..."

"No, Butter, no. It's my job to put you through college. No loans, no grants, no government shit. You won't need it, now case closed!" Trey shouted.

Butter lay across the bed and felt the tears start to roll down her face. Trey lay down beside her, feeling bad for raising her voice at her. Butter just didn't understand. School wasn't for everybody and she wasn't built for the college life.

Government handouts had been a part of Trey and Pebbles' life all too often growing up. After Trey's father was sent to prison, from welfare to food stamps to government cheese, Trey had seen enough. She would do whatever it took to pay for Butter and Pebbles' education herself--no "poor peoples' aid".

She understood that Butter only wanted what was best for her, but Butter failed to realize that, to Trey, it meant getting both her and Pebbles away from the 'hood for good. They never belonged there and she wanted nothing more than to see them succeed outside St. Louis. Then to her, all this hustling, robbing and stealing wouldn't all be in vain.

She slowly ran her fingers through Butter's hair. "I'm sorry, baby, I shouldn't have raised my voice. I just need to handle you and Pebbles' tuition first. Then..."

Trey's phone began to vibrate and Butter's sighed. "Can't you ignore it just this one day?" Trey kissed her both deeply and passionately and shook her head.

"Might be money, baby, and the sooner I clock cash, the sooner I get ya'll out of here."

Butter reclined on her pillow as Trey spoke on the phone. When she hung up, her face was tossed and angry.

"What is it, baby? What's wrong, Trey?"

"Nothing, just some shit I found out about ol' boy Pebbles' workin' for that I don't like. Look, baby, I gotta go see somebody. I'll be back in a few," Trey said, gathering her things. As she leaned in to kiss Butter goodbye she was met with opposition.

"Trey, I can't believe you had the man investigated. Ya'll tried to rob him, remember? Besides, Pebbles is a grown ass woman. She can take care of herself."

Butter hated the way that Trey felt she always had to protect Pebbles. She understood that they grew up together, more like sisters than cousins, but Butter was tired of the way Trey dropped everything at the drop of a dime to run to Pebbles' rescue.

"Look, Butta, I can't get into this with you right now. I gotta jet. I'll be back."

Trey headed out the door and Butter lay there wondering where her future was heading. The Clit was bound to get Trey into some shit not even "Queen B" April Clyne could get her out of. She wondered if college was a realistic dream depending on Trey alone.

I gotta take care of myself. I can't keep relying on Trey. Hell, at the rate she's going, she'll be doing time in no time.

Butter reached over into her Gucci bag on the floor and flipped through her phone book. When she saw his name, memories came flooding back--some good, some bad. The good ones were enough to make her pick up the phone and start dialing.

Chapter Eight

When she heard his car door close, Pebbles was lying on the couch in the living room, exhausted. Hard to believe she achieved this level of fatigue by simply cleaning one room. *Shit, I ain't gon' make it! I can't take this! Soon as he gets in this damn house, I'm a tell him to take this funky job and shove it!*

When the door opened, she hurried to her feet and pretended to be washing the huge bay window. When Xavier rounded the corner, she began an utterance that was quickly interrupted by the sight of all the blood on his shirt. "Oh my God! You're bleeding! Are you okay? Are you hurt? What happened to you? Do you need me to call 911 for you?"

Xavier held up his hands to calm her. "No, I don't need an ambulance, I'm not hurt, at least not physically anyway."

He walked over to the couch, sat down and began unbuttoning his shirt. Pebbles nervously came to sit beside him. "Well, why do you have all this blood on your shirt?"

Xavier stared off into space and sat silent for a moment. "A very good friend of mine was killed today. Right beside me in the same car."

Outdone by what he'd said, all Pebbles could offer was, "Damn! That's fucked up. I didn't know that kinda shit went down out here."

"We were boys for seven years and I seen him get his head splattered all over the windshield in front of my very own eyes and I couldn't do shit about it."

Pebbles subconsciously placed her hand upon his lap. She felt bad for him. "I know how you feel."

Xavier looked to her hand and then to her. Her hand was soft and felt so warm to his skin. "And how would you know what I feel?"

"Cause I actually live in the 'hood, unlike you. I've seen many people die in front of me and there would be nothing I could do to neither help them nor have prevented it. It is nothing more painful to see than an innocent child lying in the street, covered in blood because they were hit by a stray bullet while playing in front of their own damn house."

Xavier nodded his head in agreement. "You're right, I apologize. Well," he said as he rose from the couch. He thought about staying in that one spot all day, just for her hand to remain upon his lap but he decided against it. "I'd better hit the shower."

"Okay," Pebbles said as she wiped her sweaty palms on the front of her jeans. She lustfully admired the six pack underneath his shirt before offering her condolences once again.

"Thanks," he said, walking towards the stairs. "By the way, what's for lunch?" he asked almost afraid of the answer, remembering breakfast.

Pebbles hunched her shoulders in confusion. "I don't know. I'm still on this living room.

"From three hours ago?" He waved his hand. "Never mind, forget lunch."

He turned to walk up the stairs as Pebbles called out to him. "Will your wife be home soon?"

Xavier stopped mid-step and exhaled an irritated sigh and spun towards her with an impatient look on his face for all the questions concerning his wife. Yet she hadn't known so he couldn't fault her. He figured he may as well tell her.

He glanced at the picture of the two of them together outlined by the beautiful gold frame Stephanie had purchased. "LaShey, my wife is dead."

Pebbles dropped the bottle of spray cleaner from her hand and placed it over her mouth. She only wished she could dig her foot out first.

"She died a couple years back."

"I'm sorry. I...I didn't know..."

"Well, now you do. No more questions."

Xavier turned and proceeded up the stairs, only to holler back a message for Pebbles. "By the way, the next time you clean the windows, you might wanna use Windex, not Fantastic. It's tile cleaner."

That would explain the cloud of circular strokes on the window, Pebbles thought to herself. She plopped back down on the couch, praying the day would quickly come to an end. *Dead! Damn, and you still got her clothes and shit in the closet. Now that's love!*

••••••

For the first time that day, Xavier chuckled to himself. *Fantastic! God, help me!*

He stripped down his clothes and turned on the shower. He sat naked on his king sized bed and made the call he knew would make him feel better.

Patricia, Stephanie's mom, answered on the first ring. "Hey Ma!"

Delight filled the receiver as she welcomed his call. "I thought you dropped dead, son."

Xavier felt a tinge in his spine as he thought back to Pedro. "I almost did."

"Say again?"

Xavier began to fill her in on all the happenings of the past few days. "Sounds like you've definitely been busy. God has certainly watched over you, son. You know, Xavier, I was thinking about you the other day. I know it was you and Piggy's anniversary and I was wondering how you were. Now I feel so bad for not calling and checking on you. However, I am glad you didn't take that Sasha on that trip. I don't care much for her, you know that. She got 'gold digger' written all across her forehead. I wish you'd get rid of her and find someone better. Someone who deserves you..."

Her words faded as Xavier lay back on the black silk comforter and thought of Pebbles downstairs. He smirked again. Her hand felt so gentle to him. Her touch had soothed him. He enjoyed it, maybe a little too much. Thoughts of her made his penis rock hard and he didn't fight it.

"Oh shit, I'm sorry!"

Xavier jumped as Pebbles came flying into the room. He threw a pillow across his hardness, embarrassed by her presence.

"I'm sorry, I heard the shower and I was coming to get those bloody clothes and throw them away. I...thought you were in the...oh shit! I'm sorry."

"Calm down, its cool."

Xavier excused himself from the phone with Patricia and hung up.

"I should go," Pebbles said, thinking she was walking backwards but not taking a step, her eyes glued to the pillow, secretly wishing he'd move it again.

Finally, he gestured to the door and she snapped back to reality.

"Oh, sorry!"

When the door closed, he stood immediately to lock it, leaving the pillow behind. Inches away from the knob, it re-opened.

"Look, I..."

They stood there, inches apart, him naked, she dazed. He could feel the heat between them. Pebbles swallowed hard, looked down without hesitation and took in every inch of his penis. Her mouth began to water and the muscles inside her vagina began to tighten. *Damn his dick is big...and beautiful!* she thought. *An array of beautiful colors. Blended colors of browns and topped off with a shade of pink.*

"You were saying?" Xavier asked. He longed to grab her right there and unleash his buried passion for her. It turned him on the way she looked at him. But it wouldn't be anything but a cheap fling and could cost him more in the long run. He had learned a long time ago to not mix business with pleasure.

Xavier didn't move, allowing her to take in all of him, just as he'd done the night he saw her in the closet. He wanted her to have the same thoughts, dreams, and desires. He could see it in her eyes, she already had.

"I... I..." she sighed "I don't know what the hell I was finna say. I..."

"Its okay, we're even," he said, closing the door. He locked it and smiled.

Pebbles stood on the other side, insides turning like crazy. "Damn, he fine!" she whispered. "Damn!"

••••••

The water was running down his back, the steam rising from the flow. She placed her arms around his waist and slowly rubbed them up his chest. Her tongue glided up his back to his neck, making him weak in the knees. Her hands moved down his stomach and found his penis…so strong, so solid...a warrior on the hunt for release.

She stepped in front of him. The water was now beating down upon her back. The chill on the front of her body made her nipples rise. He leaned in, engulfed one into his mouth, his free hand finding its way between her thighs. Her sighs got deep as he thrust inside her like a mad man. He wanted to bring her to her knees.

Quickly and forcefully he fingered her until she screamed for him to stop, begged him to enter her with his penis. He lifts her leg onto the rim of the tub to grant him the access he desires. She drops her head back to let the water beat down upon her face. Within seconds he could feel the muscles inside her tighten and her moans become more operatic. He has accomplished his goal.

He turns her away from him, places her leg back upon the rim and fights his way inside her. She's hotter that the water on the inside. He gyrates his hips to a rhythm he knows will drive her insane. Turned on by the view of her ass, he reaches for her hair and begins to thrust harder. Wants to punish her for the way he thinks of her, the way he desires her...the way he needs her.

Bending at the knees and climbing deeper and deeper with every blow, the hot water running down the crease of her butt onto his penis intensifies the pleasure within her walls. She screams for him to go faster.

"Give it to me, baby! Fuck me harder! Come on, baby! Yeah...that's it! Harder!"

He gripped her ass with a death lock on her cheeks and plunged into her as hard as he could. Her womb welcomed the challenge of his penis as he played a rhythmic drum pattern on her cervix. "Come for Xav, baby! That's right, come for me!"

Her back arches, he grips her around the waist to hold her up and rips inside her. Her screams become more vocal, her body orgasmic like never before. His flesh, ready to follow suit, overheats. He makes his requests known to her. "Drink it!"

She turned around and dropped to her knees. Urgently, she began to deep throat him as he pumped his passion into her throat.

He is relieved, he is relaxed…and he is...standing alone in the shower, sperm running down his inner thighs, his hand--tired from the journey into masturbation.

He is upset with himself for feeling so attracted to her. Tells himself he needs to get away from her and get his mind right. *I can't stay around Pebbles to long. Too much inside, too much desire, too much want...too much, like Stephanie!*

Chapter Nine

Trey pulled up to the familiar mansion on Sherman Oaks Road. *What the hell have I gotten her into? I should've never let her come with us.*

She cut off the engine and stepped outside the car. Her stomach tied in knots as she envisioned seeing the owner of the house again. She'd left her gun in the car and felt and irritating sense of vulnerability. She hated being naked without her nine.

When she reached the door, she rang the bell praying it would be "the maid" who answered.

Pebbles swung open the door and gave Trey the greeting from hell. "What the hell are you doing here? You alone? Ya'll better not be tryin' no bullshit. What the hell is you at this man's house for in broad daylight?"

Trey stepped back and ran her fingers around her lips as she always did when she was trying to figure out the best way to approach a situation.

"Ain't nobody on no bullshit, a'ight? I'm by myself. Now calm yo' ass down and get out here. I need to holla at you."

Pebbles looked over her shoulder and then back to Trey. "Make it quick."

When the door closed, Trey lit into her with fury. "Who the fuck are you now, the guard dog? How the fuck you gon' play me like that? You think I'd jeopardize you like that? I've had yo' back from day one and I drove all the way out here in the fuckin' boondocks 'cause I still got it. Now calm yo' ass down and let me tell you what I came to tell you. This Winston nigga, Pebbles, baby, this nigga ain't who you think he is."

Pebbles stepped back, threw her hand over her mouth and said sarcastically, "Oh, my God! You mean he ain't the rich ass, fine ass nigga we just tried to rob the other night?"

Trey frowned at Pebbles for being cute. "Very fuckin' funny. His ass is rich a'ight, but it ain't from no damn football team. Pebbs, his ass is movin' weight, real weight. And I don't want you near him nor this fuckin' house. I know this job got us out of that case but yo' safety ain't worth this shit. I don't know, I'll get a lawyer or somethin' but you can't stay here. You been in enough shit and you ain't about to get in any mo'. So, get yo' shit and lets go."

Pebbles rolled her eyes and thought about what Trey had just told her. *He balls? Damn, he fine as hell and got some thug in him? She must be out her damn mind if she think I'm leavin' this.*

Pebbles looked at Trey, who was standing at the bottom of the steps looking up at Pebbles like, "*now!*" Pebbles frowned and waved her hand. She wasn't leaving, especially after what she felt between them in the bedroom. She was sure there was an attraction that existed between them. She felt it, she was sure of it. So Trey would just have to be upset 'cause her feet were planted and she wasn't uprooting them any time soon. Yet, she couldn't tell Trey all of that, so she played the prison card.

"Fo' what? So he can have both of us locked back up? Trey, what kinda shit is that? You wanna see me go back to jail, 'cause I damn sure don't wanna see you go back. Especially if I could have done somethin' to have prevented it. You talk all this tough ass talk but you would sacrifice and do the same shit for me, I know you would. I'm not leaving, Trey. I gotta do this."

"Did you hear me? This nigga is dealin', Pebbs. Look around you. With this much clout, he ain't dealin' no petty shit. Now, I said I don't want you around this shit."

"Why not? I'm around you when you do it, Trey."

Trey's blood began to boil and she was getting irritated with Pebbles' stubbornness. "Ain't that a bitch! I would die for you at the drop of a dime, Pebbles, you know that. Would he? Fuck naw! I keep you with me and close to me 'cause I can and I will always protect you. Now cut the bullshit and lets bounce."

Trey grabbed her arm and Pebbles pulled away and reached back to open the door. "Look, Trey. I ain't going no where 'til six o'clock. Now if you wanna sit in that raggedy ass car and wait on me, I'll be out in about, oh, say two-to-three hours. Other than that, I'll holla back. I'm a big girl, Trey, and I can handle this, so chill."

"A'ight, big girl," Trey said, sucking her teeth. "Yo' ass wasn't so big the other night now was you, all that cryin' and shit." She threw up her hand. "You shol' right. Fuck it, I'm out!"

Trey turned to walk away and Pebbles felt bad. Pebbles knew that Trey was only trying to look out for her like she had always done. But Pebbles thought that Trey had to learn to let her grow up and handle shit on her own. She jumped down the steps and ran down the walkway to catch Trey.

"Trey! Trey, I'm sorry. My bad. I know you just being blue, but I'm cool, Trey, really. Try to understand that I'm doing this for both of us. I ain't tryin' to see you go up for ten plus years on that gun shit and a probation violation. I need you to trust me and believe me when I tell you I'm cool. If anything feels crazy to me, you know I'll pick up the phone and call you without hesitation, okay? Now, I gotta go before he sees me out here talkin' to you and think I'm tryin' to cross him. I'll call you as soon as I get home. Promise."

Trey sighed and nodded her head. She kissed Pebbles on her cheek and headed for the car. She turned back to issue Pebbles one final warning. "A'ight, but you betta watch that nigga. He do anything, Pebbs, I mean anything that could remotely hurt you in any way, I'ma kill that nigga and you know I mean that."

"Yeah, I know."

Pebbles waved goodbye and turned back to the house. *Watch him? She'd love to.*

Trey jumped in her '78 Cutlass and sped off. She called East-Bay and told him to keep his ear to the ground concerning Xavier and to call her at the smallest buzz of negative street talk.

She popped 2Pac in the CD player, hit the highway and thought of Butter, as the Pied Piper laid it down: "*...Yo' fantasies come alive, yo' heart rate shall increase when we meet up in this dark place. You might think you happy with him but that's a lie, so give this thug a try. I'd rather be yo' N-I-G-G-A, so we can get drunk and smoke weed all day. It don't matter if you lonely baby, you need a thug in yo' life, them bustas ain't lovin' you right...*".

Trey shook her head and laughed as she thought of Butter, probably at home waiting to make good love to her. *Here I am, out here tryin' to be captain save-a-hoe and I could be at home gettin' broke off. What the hell is wrong with this picture?*

••••••

"I'm down," Lilac replied after Queen laid down her plan to use Pebbles to finish off Xavier. "Lilac, this nigga own a liquor store and a pawnshop. We fucked up and we hit him the wrong way. Bump the house, we should have went fo' the stores. We get the alarm codes from Pebbles and all is sweet with the world."

Lilac thought of how that would implicate Pebbles, therefore she knew Trey wouldn't go along with it.

"You think Trey gon' go for that?"

"Fuck Trey! She don't wanna handle business, we'll go at it without her. I'm sure Pebbs can be persuaded. I gotta lil' somethin' for that ass."

"A'ight, set it up and get back at me. Moms got me stickin' to her like glue since I got bailed out. I gotta take her to the grocery store. I'll holla back."

Queen placed a few calls to put her plan in motion. Pebbles would go along by force if necessary. Queen wasn't down for goin' to prison and not have shit to show for it.

In order for a man to have somethin' he has never had before, he must do somethin' he has never done before, she thought to herself. She had never thought of crossing any of her crew members before, but things were getting hectic out there and Queen felt she needed to step her game up.

To run smoothly, her plan would take grip, which meant she had to quit lounging around and get her hustle on. The planned outcome gave her both motivation and inspiration. After it all went down, her reputation would never be the same in the 'hood.

••••••

"I heard the doorbell a minute ago," Xavier asked as he walked into the living room. He was truly bewildered that she was still cleaning that same damn room. "Umm, are you afraid to leave this room or somethin'?"

She put up her hand, palm to his direction. "Ha, ha. No, I'm just takin' my time, makin' sure I get it right."

"I see. And the doorbell?"

"Girl Scouts," she lied. She didn't need him thinking that she was plotting on him by saying it was Trey.

"Order any?" he asked, knowing she wasn't being truthful.

She turned to him. "Any what?"

He chuckled, amazed that she was so thoughtfully challenged. "Cookies. You know, Girl Scouts--cookies/cookies--Girl Scouts."

"I started to, for your dinner and all, but I decided against it."

Mimicking Pebbles, Xavier placed his hand on his hip and frowned, "Ha, ha."

The doorbell rang again and Pebbles stomach did somersaults. Xavier smiled and said, "Persistent little creatures, aren't they?"

As he disappeared around the corner, her heart sped up. He popped his head back inside the room. "You ordered pizza?"

She had almost forgotten. With a sigh of relief she smiled. "Pizza, yeah, for us...umm I mean for an early dinner...so...you wouldn't be hungry."

Xavier disappeared around the corner, paid for the pizza and returned to the living room. Pebbles' pulse finally returned to normal. She felt so antsy around him. She wanted to ask him about the things that Trey had said concerning his lifestyle but she decided against it. It would just put him on the defensive again.

He walked over to the black marbled bar and drew two glasses. "Drink?"

"Okay, yeah. Whatever you're having, I'll have."

"I don't think so," Xavier said raising an eyebrow and heading to the kitchen. You're too young to have what I'm having. Milk?"

She launched a corner of pizza across the room before she realized it, hitting him in the upper chest. Xavier stepped back and looked at her. He couldn't believe what she had just done, although secretly, he admired her spunk.

She jumped off the couch and grabbed a handful of napkins. "Oh shit! I'm sorry. I forgot where I was. I'm sorry. Please don't fire me."

He picked the meat from his chest and smiled. "Naw, but the way you cook around here, I'd betta save this for breakfast tomorrow."

She punched him in the arm and they both burst out laughing.

Pebbles took her hand and removed the onion from his chin. He stared into her eyes. He was mesmerized by her beauty--captivated by her innocence. "Why?"

She looked at him, puzzled.

"Why did you and your friends try to rob me blind?"

Pebbles immediately became defensive. "Why you gotta go there? I mean, damn, I said I was sorry. Are you ever gonna let me live that down?"

"So what else do you do besides tryin' to be a new millennium cat burglar, which you're not to good at by the way. I know it ain't cookin' or cleanin'."

That brought a smile out of her and she began to laugh.

For the next couple of hours, Pebbles told him about her life--school, her parents, her grandmother and The Clit. She explained the situation concerning her mother, and Xavier felt unexplainably uneasy. He couldn't understand why that name had brought him such disturbing feelings. But until he could find out more about her and her incarceration, Xavier wouldn't press the questions concerning her.

Pebbles went on to talk about her closeness to Trey and their affiliation to The Clit. "In the 'hood, you have to belong. Its clique up or suffer the consequences."

Xavier found her quite interesting and was really enjoying her company, maybe a little too much. She took his mind off the Brooklyn roughnecks, Pedro and Stephanie. She made him laugh, something he didn't do that often.

"So, I've told you about me but you haven't said a word about you."

"It's my job as your employer to know as much as I can about you, knowing where you hang out in case I come home one day and you cleaned me out." He rose off the sofa to refill his glass of Hypnotic.

"So why the football team?"

She was sitting on the couch looking so sexy to him. He liked talking about his business adventures with someone, especially someone he was attracted too. He needed to leave but he couldn't bring himself to do so at that moment. He was drawn to her. "Why not? Can you think of a better booming industry in St. Louis right now?"

"Is that all you own?"

Xavier looked at her suspiciously. "I don't own it, I have stock in it and no more questions about my business. Now, I gotta go out. I'll be back late. If you're gone, I'll see you back first thing in the morning."

"You really think you should be driving? You've had four of those already."

"Ohhh, I didn't know you cared!" he said as he exited the room.

Pebbles bent down to answer her phone. It was Queen. "What's up?"

"What's up is I need to holla you about ol' boy," Queen said. Pebbles lay back on the couch, annoyed.

"I already know. Trey told me. So he sells dope. I don't care how he pays me, as long as it keeps me outta jail. It's no big deal, I'm cool."

Queen couldn't believe what she was hearing. *He balls?* Her day was getting brighter and brighter by the moment. "Naw, that ain't it. Call me when you get home, it's important, a'ight?"

"A'ight."

Pebbles wondered what else Queen could have to tell her concerning Xavier as she cleaned up the mess they had made. She was also wondering what was taking him so long to leave. *Maybe he'll let me leave early and drop me off at the Metrolink on his way out.*

She headed up the stairs to his bedroom. When she knocked on the door and got no answer, she got worried. She opened the door to find him lying on the bed, half dressed. She shook her head. *Let me find out this nigga can't hold his liquor!*

She walked over to the bed and began removing his shoes.

••••••

As the phone rang on the other side of the line, and her ear anxiously glued to the phone, Butter slowly began to have second thoughts. It was not her intention to hurt Trey in anyway, she just needed a back up plan, a Plan B.

"Holla!" his voice crooned through the receiver. She sat silently as he again greeted the caller.

"Hello, Jayson!" It was all she could muster up. The hair on her body stood erect as her stomach sprang with butterflies.

"Is that… naw, I know that ain't my baby, Leslie! How you doin', shorty? I was just thinking about you the other night."

"Oh really? And why was that? Couldn't find any of the other hoochies you were cheatin' on me with?"

He chuckled. "A'ight, I deserved that. But naw, that wasn't it. I was over at Applebee's out in St. Clair and naturally my mind went to you. "

Butter smiled as she thought back to their last dinner at her favorite restaurant. The tables were draped with long, fancy tablecloths and Jayson kept playing between her thighs, so she decided to give him a run for his money.

When the waiter left, she slipped underneath the table, unzipped his pants and gave a hummer job right there in the restaurant. His mind was blown by her boldness and spontaneity. She would have paid any amount of money to have a camera and capture the look on his face as he tried to order dinner. The more he tried to speak, the more she teased the head of his jimmy. Right as he was about to blow, his legs began to shake and he lost his breath. As she relieved him, the stutter in his speech made it evident to the waiter what was going on. He told Jayson he'd be back later.

"Yeah, we had some good times at good ol' Applebee's," she laughed. Silence fell among them.

"So, what's up, Miss Lady?"

"I just called to touch bases, that's all. See how you were doing."

He snickered. "Now you know I know better than that. What's really good? Rubbin' clits ain't doin' it for you no more?"

"That ain't it. I...I need a favor."

"Oh, you need me now. You didn't need me when you packed up, killed my baby and left me fo' that lil' nigga-wanna-be."

Butter angered quickly. "As I recall, I wasn't the only one you had knocked up. I was one of three. So, don't come off like you were so innocent."

"That shouldn't have mattered. I'm a man. I do what I wanna do and always what I need to do. As long as you was taken care of, nothing else should've mattered. Them hoes didn't mean nothing to me. Convenient pussy. You, you was my heart. You was my Butta, but you chose a bitch over me, made me look like less than a man in front of my crew, and now you want a favor?"

Butter was regretting she even dialed his number. He had a point, she had no business calling him let alone asking him for money. "You're right, Jayson, this was a mistake. Take care."

She heard him call her name as she removed the phone from her ear. "What is it you need?"

"Money...for school."

"How much we talkin'?"

"Just enough for the first semester, maybe the second. To hold me down while...well, until I get a job."

"Total?"

"About five to six-thousand."

He was silent, asking himself was she worth it. "What you gon' do for me?"

It was the question she knew would eventually come. "What is it you want me to do, Jayson?"

"You know what time it is. Holla at me tomorrow, I'll have it for you, a'ight? A'ight?"

She hung up the phone just as Trey walked in the front door. She called out to Butter to come into the living room. When she entered, Butter's face lit up as she looked at the balloons and roses on the table.

Trey walked over to her, put her arms around her and kissed her. "I missed you today. You missed me?"

"You know I did," Butter said running her fingers down Trey's back and gripping her butt. "Aey, I told you 'bout touching my ass."

Butter pulled Trey closer and told her to follow her to the bedroom which Trey, without hesitation, obeyed.

Chapter Ten

It startled her when he reached for her. She had already removed his shoes, socks and his shirt. Her trembling hands found her way to his belt buckle and unsnapped his jeans. Her eyes cooed at the fine grade of hair he had and she ran across it with her fingers.

Her heart almost stopped when his hand touched hers. Only it wasn't a grip that protested her presence. It was inviting, inviting her to continue, to go beyond the borders and find him, find his erection and feel him.

Pebbles swallowed hard, unzipped his jeans and allowed her hands to search out and find his hardness lying along side his thigh. It jumped at her touch and his voice acknowledged her with a moan.

My God! she thought to herself. *It's even bigger than it looked earlier.*

Xavier rose up and through blurred vision saw the vision of loveliness that continuously appeared in his dreams.

She searched his eyes for approval and reassuringly found it there. She felt nervous and on edge. He took his hand and brushed his fingers through the silky strands if her hair. He placed a palm full to his nose and inhaled.

"Ummm, still smells so fresh."

Pebbles still had one hand upon his shaft. She didn't know where else to place it, didn't know if he wanted her to touch him all over his body or simply do the business at hand, or if he wanted passion or distance, to make love or simply fuck.

Xavier ran his hands up her arms, down her waist and under her shirt. There he found the softest set of breasts he'd ever felt. Pebbles bit her bottom lip and moaned. His hands felt so strong and intense. She reached to pull her top off he grabbed her hands. "I'll do that."

She smiled. She raised her arms as he pulled off her top followed by her bra. She stood as he pulled her pants and thong to the floor. The scent of her body seemed so familiar to him. He ran his tongue up the front of her thigh as he lifted her feet free from her clothing. "Intoxicating," he whispered as he deeply inhaled the aroma flowing from her secret garden. He reached out with his tongue and nuzzled on her clit. It was huge and erect.

He closed his eyes and got lost inside her lips, stirring his tongue around inside her. She lay back on the bed and began to spasm. Her back arched, her thighs tightened and her toes locked. She moaned intensely as she freely let her desire for him be known. He slid up her thighs and leaned in to kiss her.

"I always loved the way your body jerked when you cum."

Pebbles looked confusingly to him and asked, "What do you mean by 'always'?"

He didn't verbally respond. He answered as he pressed inside her with his hardness, causing her to quiver inside. He was long and strong and Pebbles lost all thought of reality as he raised her hips and buried himself deeply underneath her pelvis.

Their bodies mingled, tongues intertwined, hips thrust and gyrated together. She panted and came, came and panted. She gripped his back and rode him from underneath, locking her legs around his.

She matched each stroke with her own, grinding on the tip of his jimmy each time he pulled out. She glanced up, loving the way the sweat dripped from his face. He was putting in work to make her feel good. That made her want to please him even more.

"You want to switch positions?"

Xavier shook his head "no" as he began to stroke deeper and deeper. He raised her legs back to her chest and was granted clear access to her waterfall of love.

"You know this is my favorite position," he panted.

"Xavier, wait...wait...!"

She wanted him to stop. She needed him to stop. Something was very wrong here. But the more she protested, the more he plunged inside her and the more she got off.

Finally, the heat of her body had overcome his will. He wanted this dream to never end. He fought and fought, but in the end, he lost the battle as what seemed like gallons of need pumped down underneath her womb. He moaned, he shook, he whispered, "Umm, Stephanie...oh, baby! God, I've missed you!"

Pebbles was crushed in an instant. She wanted to break beneath him but refused to do so. He lay still, breathing both labored and heavy. She lay there with him until he had fallen asleep. She slid from below him, quietly gathered her things, cleaned up in his bathroom and returned to his bedroom. She stood there staring down at him. *He thought I was her! I don't believe this shit. The whole damn time, he thought I was her! How fuckin' stupid am I?*

She picked up the covers and threw them across his naked body. She gathered his clothing and took them down to the laundry area, then she returned to make sure that no traces of her remained behind. She took one last glance before she exited the room, shut the door and cried.

••••••

Queen had had a good night on the hustling end. She'd clocked enough grip to move forward with her plan. She sat on her full sized bed and stared up at the bold traveling creature making its way across her favorite DMX poster. She down bent and picked up her house shoe, walked over to the wall and swatted the roach sending it to the floor. "Can't wait to get the hell outta this dump."

She swatted another as she reached for her phone. "Yeah, yeah!" she answered, plopping back down upon the bed.

"It's Pebbles. What was so important?"

"What's up Pebbs? Where you at?"

Pebbles lied and told her she was downtown waiting on the bus when the truth was, she was still out in St. Charles. She wasn't in the mood to be questioned about her whereabouts.

"Well, I been thinking, and I found out a way for you to pay for college. We got some information on ol' boy I think you might find interesting."

"Like what?" Pebbles asked.

"That nigga own a pawnshop and a liquor store. I think we can take 'em if we plan it right. We can get enough to get off these cases and do some thangs."

"Queen, are you out of yo' damn mind? You don't think he'll be a tad bit suspicious that I start working for him and his businesses get jacked? He already watchin' my ass like a hawk.

No way, count me out and any assistance you thought you were gon' get from me. Did you run this shit by Trey?"

Queen inhaled her blunt and frowned. "Man, Trey ain't down either. Why ya'll bitchin' up over this nigga? 'Cause he dropped the charges against ya'll? Let me find out its some twisted shit in the game."

"Naw, ain't shit twisted. I'm tryin' to go to school. I ain't got time fo' that shit. That night in jail woke my ass straight the fuck up and I'm always down fo' yo' ass, I just ain't goin' to jail fo' yo' ass."

Pebbles saw her train coming in the distance. She sighed with relief, knowing she'd have to end her call with Queen. "Look, my bus is here. I'll holla at you later."

Queen clicked the phone without saying a word. She was in enraged. "I'm so sick of these bitches!" she said as she dialed Lilac's number.

When Lilac answered, Queen simply spoke, "Plan B."

Lilac knew immediately what that meant. She rolled over and dozed back off to sleep knowing she had a full plate to digest the following day.

Queen lit up another blunt, turned up her sound system, blasting her favorite MC of the new day. As she puffed away in frustration, Murphy Lee laced the track. "*...It be them same ol' clowns, giving you pound, pretending they down, but when you leave town they go around runnin' they mouths...*".

She couldn't understand why Pebbles would even agree to take that job and not just ride it out with the rest of the crew. She was just as disappointed in Trey. They looked out for themselves in the situation and that spelled disloyalty to Queen.

She thought back to the night they all went to watch Jada and the crew *Set It Off* in the theater. They vowed to stick together no matter what, thick or thin. But when the shit got tight, Pebbles and Trey had their own agenda.

"So now, maybe I ought to have mine," she said as she stomped the 3-D sized roach crawling across the floor. "Fuckin' roaches got mo' heart than these bitches!"

Chapter Eleven

Xavier awoke with a headache from hell. The small buzz of the alarm clock magnified intensely. He reached over and slammed off the constant drumbeat and rolled over. His hand found his nakedness below his waist. He rose his head and peeked under the satin spread. *What the fuck!* He sprang up searching his mind for some sort of remembrance of the previous night. Vaguely, he remembered having pizza with Pebbles and having a few glasses of Hypnotic, but any occurrence after that was a total blur to him. He looked around for his clothing only to find that they were all missing. He stood to his feet and felt sick to his stomach. He raced to the toilet and began to hurl, his head feeling a slight relief once he was done.

As he stood and relieved his bladder he stretched and thought about Pebbles. He could smell her, feel her...taste her. She was all around him and he didn't understand why. He slapped his hand to his head and tried to focus once again on the night before. He'd drank a lot but surely he'd remember being with her, especially her. Was it her who undressed him? *It had to be. Naw, it couldn't be!*

He reached over and turned on the shower. He grabbed the remote and hit the built in wall unit in the bathroom and turned on the morning news. Pedro's death was mentioned as a robbery and attempted car jacking:

"*...Also in the car but unharmed was Xavier Winston, a local businessman who owned the liquor store...*".

Immediately, the phone began to ring. He allowed the answering machine to pick up. The first call was from Stephanie's mother, Patricia, expressing her love and concern again. The second was from Sasha.

"Oh, baby, I am so sorry for the other day sweetie. Can you call me right away? I'm so worried about you. I love you, honey. Bye!"

He shut the bathroom door and stepped into the shower. He had no immediate plans for the day. The car show in Forest Park didn't start until 3 P.M. He realized that now that he was a legitimate businessman, he'd have a lot more time on his hands.

He dressed and headed downstairs to answer the outside gate. When Pebbles reached the door, he was already waiting for her.

"Morning," he said to her, walking towards the kitchen. "Let's see what room you'll clean today," he chuckled.

She flipped him the bird and set the bag of donuts down on the kitchen counter top.

"Those donuts?"

"Only the best. They're from over on Cass and Grand Avenue. Best twists in the city."

She looked at him and felt a strong tingle in her spine. He was so handsome in his Phem throw back jersey and matching Phem cap. His skin was smooth, and his goatee fleshly shaved. They sat at the table to eat.

Xavier looked across to her, astonished by her beauty. Her hair was pulled back into a brown decorated clip with spikes on top. Her makeup was radiant.

"So, what time did you leave last night?"

Pebbles looked at him, caught off guard. She simply couldn't believe he didn't remember the night before.

"Around seven-thirty. Why?"

"Damn, it took you that long to clean the living room?" He laughed. "At that rate, the whole house won't be cleaned 'til next month!"

Pebbles tried to swallow her food but it felt as if her throat was swollen shut. She wiped her mouth and asked the question she was afraid to hear him answer.

"You don't remember last night at all?"

Xavier shook his head. He was dumbfounded. "Is there a particular reason I should?"

It was bad enough that he'd made love to her thinking she was his dead wife, but for him not to remember at all! The act itself, forgotten! Her heart sank as she gathered her wits and tried to stay composed. She had sat up all night thinking about it, how he felt, how his touch was like none she'd ever felt before, yet she would humiliate herself no further.

"No, no reason. You just drank a little too much and you were supposed to be on your way out. You went upstairs to change. I came to let you know I was leaving but you were laid out on the bed, butt ass naked. I threw your cover across you, grabbed your clothes and headed home."

"Oh no, my bad! I usually don't drink like that. But yesterday was kind of hectic and shit. Taking care of yo' drunk ass boss in not in yo' job description, so I truly apologize."

"No problem," she said, heating him up another donut and refilling his glass of milk.

"Let me make it up to you."

"Make up what?"

"You staying late. Forest Park is having a car show sponsored by 104.9 FM. I hear its gonna be off the hook. Nelly's 'pose to perform. You...you wanna...would you like to go?"

"Me...go with you? To Forest Park?"

"Is there an echo in here? Yeah, that's what I said."

Just yesterday, she would have jumped at the chance to be seen in public, especially in the 'hood with a brother as fine as Xavier. But yesterday was before she'd slept with him and felt so invisible behind it.

"Naw, but thanks anyway. I...I really need to study for finals. I brought my books with me. Plus, I need to get the laundry done."

Xavier admired her desire to study and arose from the table promising her he'd try to get Nelly's autograph for her as a way of thanking her. He went into the living room and called down to Ted Foster's Funeral Home to make arrangements for Pedro's burial before heading out to pick up his spare tire choice for the day.

Sasha was all too happy to hear he'd be over. Xavier resented her for always willing to be second choice in his life. She cared about nothing but his money. *Maybe that's what seems so attractive about LaShey,* he thought to himself. *She seems so simple and unaffected by what I got.*

...One more thing that reminded him of the love of his life. One more thing that also reminded him to back off...!

••••••

Queen called Trey and she headed out early that morning. Butter showered and called Jayson. They agreed to meet at the downtown Adams Mark Hotel at two. Butter knew she had at least until eight that evening because Trey was going to the car show with Queen later that afternoon.

As Butter dressed, she contemplated normal things, such as putting on body spray, perfume, etc. She didn't want Jayson to think that this was anything other than what it was, business.

She dressed in one of Trey's Nike sweat suits and pulled her hair up into a ponytail. She wore no make up besides Strawberry lip-gloss.

Second thoughts swarmed through her head all the way to Room 423. As she knocked on the door, her cell phone rang. It was Trey. If she answered, Trey would want to know where she was. As her finger moved towards the send button, the hotel door opened.

Standing before her was a 6'3, chocolate covered Jayson. He was handsome with his bald head, his eyes slanted and inviting. His chest had buffed since the last time they were together.

Butter closed the phone and returned it to her purse. She didn't know why, but at that moment, she had no interest in what Trey had to say. Could it have been the way Jayson stepped close to her and ran his hands down her cheeks to her throat? The way he placed soft kisses on her cheeks and ran his tongue down her neck? They way he placed his hands inside her sweats to find her soaking wet? Or running his palms down the front of her thighs and up the back to grip her butt cheeks?

Butter lost herself in his touch and deep in her soul began to remember what it was like to be loved by a man. Jayson pulled her inside the room and kicked the door shut with his Timbs, never releasing Butter from his grip.

"You feel so good, shorty," he whispered as he stood in front of her, hardness pressed against her.

She looked into his eyes and old feelings threatened to unravel her. She had loved him with all of her soul at one time and would have done anything for him without explanation or hesitation. But he'd hurt her deeply, a wound that hadn't completely healed, a wound that reminded her of the business at hand.

She stepped away from his grip and looked down at the floor and bit her bottom lip. "Jayson, I really need that."

Jayson nodded, walked over to the dresser, opened the drawer and retrieved the manila envelope. He held it out to Butter and whispered, "What you needed, plus a little puttin' extra."

Butter walked over to Jayson, took the envelope and opened it. As she stared down at the envelope full of fifty and one hundred-dollar bills, she felt dirty. "I feel like such a whore."

Jayson stood behind her, wrapped his arms around her waist and kissed the back of her neck. "You are never that. You a woman who goes after and gets what she wants, by any means necessary. Admirable to me. And you know whether you laid down with me or not, I would have given you the money 'cause I still got mad love for you."

She felt his rock solid shaft pressed hard against her ass. He took the envelope from her hand and placed on the dresser, ran his hands underneath her top and found her breasts. Her spine tingled as his fingers brushed against her erect nipples.

"I know you miss this, Les. You may love her, but she can't give you this. Can't hold you with hands like mines. Can't make your body shudder like I use to."

He swirled his fingers inside her. Her breathing became uneven. She wouldn't give him the satisfaction of knowing he was right. She kept her thoughts to herself and silently enjoyed the feelings he caused to rise up within her.

With her sweats snapped off, her top and bra tossed to the floor and thong pushed to the side, Jayson entered her from the back. Bent over the dresser, Butter could feel every inch of him. He wanted it that way. He wanted her to know that no toy could give her this pleasure. She'd hurt his pride by fucking a woman and he stroked his ego as he punished her with each thrust.

Her moans and screams sent chills through his body. He bent his knees and pushed his way deeper inside her. Her body began to spasm and Butter stopped fighting it.

Jayson grabbed her, pulled her up to him and gripped her breasts as she began to cum all over him. Her body grew weak and her legs shook uncontrollably as he whispered, "Jay missed you so much, baby. I missed you!"

She'd missed him too, or rather she missed the way he sexed her. Hadn't felt like this in years. However, she couldn't afford to let Jayson back into her life. Trey worshipped the ground Butter walked on, and for her to hurt Trey would make her no better than Jayson.

He slid from inside her and stared at the money on the dresser. "That was worth every penny in that envelope. If you wanna leave now, you can."

He walked over and lay down on the bed. Butter placed the envelope inside her bag. She looked over to him and the sight of him lying there with his manhood up again made her moist. She dropped the bag, slid off her thong and walked over to him. As she climbed up and placed a leg on either side of his head, it was no longer business, it was pleasure.

••••••

Trey was livid that she couldn't find Butter. *Where the fuck is she and why ain't she answering my damn call?*

Queen and Lilac had put Trey up on game regarding Xavier, and although she was pissed, she still refused to place Pebbles in jeopardy any further.

"If ya'll come up with another way to get the information on the stores, I'm down. But fo' the last time, I ain't putting' my lil' cousin in the mix of this shit, smell me?"

Queen looked up at Trey with a twisted face and inhaled her blunt. "Nigga, how else are we supposed to get the damn codes? She inside. If she work her area, we can have all his information without him even noticing she's involved. Quit treating her like she's twelve, bitch."

Trey tried to call Butter again and again and she got no answer. "Call it what you want, but unless you find another way, I'm out."

"Out of what?"

They all turned to see Pebbles approaching. "I thought you was at work. What you doin' here?" Trey asked, kissing her on the cheek.

"I was but he's out here somewhere. Asked me if I wanted to ride with him but I told him I had to study. Which I actually planned on doing until ya'll acted like it was a dire fuckin' emergency. So what's up?"

Trey shook her head and held up her hand, motioning like she was reeling in a fish. "Hold up! Bring it back in! What you mean he wanted you to come out here with him? What that got to do with yo' job?"

"Nothin', he just wanted to know if I wanted to see the car show."

Trey frowned. "I don't like that mutha..."

"Anyways," Queen interrupted. "Check it out Pebbs. That business we talked about the other night, I got a new proposition for you."

"I told you I ain't with it," Pebbles said, hopping up on the trunk of Queen's car.

"Yeah, yeah, bitch. I know what you said, but that was then and this is now. You've had some time to think about the consequences of you being in or being out. Now, I don't know what the fuck is up with you and yo' cousin over here, but we a crew. Our love and loyalty fo' and to each other is supposed to be blue. But ya'll bitchin' up at every turn," Queen said, stepping back and eyeing both Pebbles and Trey. "So, what's really goin' on?"

Pebbles flipped her and snickered. “Don’t start that shit again. Ain’t nobody rolled over on yo’ ass. I’m just tryin’ to get the fuck outta this ragedy ass city. You act like you can’t understand that. I ain’t tryin’ to be here the rest of my life.”

“Bitch, why you think you so much betta than us? You think ‘cause you a book worm and shit you can turn yo’ nose down on me?”

Queen approached Pebbles and Trey stepped between them. “A’ight, chill! Queen, we cool. Back the fuck up out her face...*now!*”

Queen looked to Trey and knew she was serious. Queen sucked her teeth and stepped back.

“I don’t know why she got a thang against ‘hood rats. Hell, her momma was one of the biggest rats around.”

Like lightening, Trey turned to face Queen. “What you say?”

Pebbles jumped off the trunk and stood beside Trey. “You don’t know shit about my momma.”

Lilac ran around the car and jumped in the middle of all of them. “Yo’, what the fuck is wrong with ya’ll? We peeps, we family. We beat down hoes outside this crew, not inside. Ya’ll need to chill the fuck out. People are starting to stare.”

Trey’s temples were bulging, fury racing in her heart. “Naw, I wanna know what she got to get off her chest concerning my auntie.”

“Shit, it ain’t me you need to be mad at. It’s that nigga ya’ll protectin’. That’s how her momma got hemmed up,” she said, looking to Pebbles. "Fuckin' with that same nigga ya'll tryin' to protect."

Pebbles brushed past Trey to Queen and said, "Come again?"

Queen leaned against the trunk of her car. "I'll let Lilac tell you what she uncovered."

Trey and Pebbles turned to Lilac and she gestured for them to sit as she began to tell them her news concerning Xavier.

"Years ago, Xavier planned a business trip to New York to re-comp his product. The highways were hot at the time and a third party gave Xavier the idea of using a mule. By using a mule, Xavier and company would load the mule's car with enough drugs to satisfy the highway troopers, which they would alert. It would make the pathway clear for Xavier and crew to bring in their product without incident, since the law would be concentrating on looking for the car with the mule."

Pebbles heart sank as she thought of her mother telling her grandmother that a Mexican guy had offered and her then boyfriend, James, five-thousand dollars to drive to New York and back, but didn't tell them there were drugs in the car. When they had gotten arrested, Pebbles' mother turned over the name of the man she had come in contact with, Pedro Nieves. Xavier was soon to follow.

However, with the slick courtroom antics of April Clyne, both walked free, leaving James and Pebbles' mother, Vivian, holding the bag. James' luggage was worth twenty-five years, and Vivian's fifteen.

Pebbles' blood boiled and she felt sick enough to die thinking back to the previous night. She wondered if he had known. That would explain the uneasy shift in his body every time she mentioned her name.

"Let's do it," she mumbled.

Trey looked at her and shook her head. "Let's not. You trippin'. You pissed off and you want to hurt him but this ain't the way. Not for you. Let me handle him."

Pebbles jumped from off the trunk. "She's *my* mother, Trey, not yours. And he's gonna pay for what he did to her."

Pebbles stormed off and looked back to Queen. "I'll get you what you need."

Queen bobbed her head and sucked her teeth. "It's on."

Trey pulled out her nine from her waist and laid it on the trunk between her and Queen. Queen looked at her and smiled. "Oh, what's that supposed to be, a threat? I didn't make her do shit."

Trey looked Queen in the eyes. "Maybe you should pick that up and handle yo' business now. 'Cause if anything happens to my cousin, you gon' wish you had."

Trey jumped off the car, grabbed her nine and walked away towards her ride. As she opened the door, she looked to Lilac, "And that's blue!"

She dialed Butter's phone again and still she got no answer. Then she pulled away and tried to catch Pebbles in the park but she had disappeared.

She dialed April's home number and left her a message, telling her that she'd be by in the morning. She needed to speak with her urgently. She circled and looked around once more for Pebbles and then headed home.

Queen and Lilac laughed once Trey was out of sight. "I told you, didn't I tell you? Once she knew what time it was, she'd be on board," Queen said.

"Yeah, but what we gon' do when she finds out it wasn't exactly the way we said it was?" Lilac questioned. She didn't really like using Pebbles, but she'd do anything to prove her undying loyalty to Queen.

"Fuck that! By then we'll be done got him and got these cases off our backs. We'll deal with her feelings then."

Lilac sat back on the back windshield and inhaled her newly lit blunt. "What about Trey?"

Queen waved across the street to some of her homeboys and slid down the trunk to go holla at them. "Fuck Trey," she spat as she strolled across the street.

Chapter Twelve

"It had been almost a week since you went to work, Pebbles. Don't you think he'll call the police?" Butter asked.

Pebbles stretched out across the foot of their bed and yawned. "If he was, he would have done it already, Butter."

She rubbed her temples. "Besides, I already gave Queen the information to his stores. I found it in a drawer inside his library computer desk. They're supposed to hit him Sunday night. That's when the most cash would be there because of weekend sales," she sighed. "It's gone too far to turn back now."

Butter stood by the window and shook her head in disbelief. "I can't believe you were that stupid to let Queen and Lilac talk you into that shit. Even after Trey went to April and got the *real* story."

"That's what I'm saying. It was too late by then. I was so pissed at him that day I found out, I went straight back to the house as if I never left and I searched until I found it. I called Queen and told her the information. Yeah, I regret it now but you and I both know if I tell him, I'm done in the 'hood. I'm labeled a rat and that don't fly in the 'hood."

The room fell silent as they both lay there rehashing in their minds two secret mistakes that could destroy those closest to them. Butter's mistake--Jayson. Pebbles'--Xavier.

As the sounds of Method Man flowed through the air, Pebbles thought of the choices she'd made under the influence of The Clit. "*...We can make war or make babies. Back when I was nothin', you made a brother feel like I was somethin'...*".

Pebbles thought to herself, "*He probably doesn't even remember we slept together.*"

Butter sprang up. "What did you just say?"

"Who? I didn't say nothin'," Pebbles said defensively. She thought she'd said that in her mind.

"Yes you did. You said he doesn't remember sleeping with you."

Pebbles felt the tears roll down her face. "It doesn't matter what I said. It's his fault still that momma's locked up. Anything he gets, he deserves."

Butter leaned in to face her. "Pebbles, listen to me. You know how it went down. It wasn't his fault. How was he to know that Pedro would choose *your* mother? How was he to know he would cross *your* path five years later? He was a balla, he handled his business, just like any other balla we know. He didn't put a gun to her head. Hell, he didn't even know her. If you pissed at anybody, you should be pissed at her and James for even taking that risk, knowing she had you at home."

Pebbles rose up off the bed and wiped her face. "Butter, she was only doing what she thought would help us. She was tryin' to make sure her family was okay."

"And so was he. He had a wife at the time. That's what you said, right?"

Pebbles shook her head. "A'ight then, he was protecting his family also. Any man, especially a balla who had April's ass at their disposal, would have done the same thing."

Butter sat down next to Pebbles and placed her arm around her shoulder. "It wasn't anything against you personally, Pebbles. It was business, the way things go down in the game. Sometimes we make sacrifices we later regret but at the time they feel necessary."

She was speaking more to herself than to Pebbles.

Trey had been furious when she returned home that Sunday and questioned Butter about her cell phone. "I called all day and you didn't answer. Where were you?"

"My aunt was rushed to the hospital and I had to take my Grams to see her. You know you can't have a phone in the hospital. I was gonna call you but you know how Grams is. I didn't feel like no speeches."

Trey did know, all to well, how her grandmother felt about their relationship, and with that she let it go and proceeded to explain Queen's news to Butter.

Butter felt bad for her affair with Jayson but only because she was confused about what she wanted in life. Jayson had stirred up things inside her she couldn't feel with Trey. She loved Trey, hard. Yet it was Trey's crazy behavior that had her unsure of their future together. That and the bomb ass loving Jayson laid on her for more than six hours.

Pebbles flung her head back and let out a deep breath. "You're right. How could he have known? Maybe I should go talk to him, tell him what I know and see what he has to say--smooth things out and go back to work."

"Sounds good to me," Butter said.

Pebbles reached for the phone, then remembered what she had given to Queen. She couldn't approach him about her mother and not tell him about what she had done.

"Oh my God, Butta! I can't go over there. He'll know I gave Queen the codes. He'll kill me!"

Butter lay back on the bed and stared up at the ceiling. "Shit!" was all she could say.

Pebbles flew out the bedroom quickly in hopes of talking Queen out of her plans. She ran out so quickly, she forgot her purse.

••••••

It was the eighth morning he'd come downstairs and not found Pebbles in the house. The last time she was there he'd asked her to the car show and she'd declined because she had to study for her exams. *Maybe that's it,* he reasoned. *Maybe it was exam time and she was swamped.* He reached in the kitchen drawer and grabbed the pad with all the contact numbers she had given him.

He dialed her cell first and got no answer. Then he called her grandmother, who told him LaShey had been home all week, hadn't attended school nor been out the house much. Xavier asked if she'd said anything concerning her job. Her grandmother told him no. Xavier thanked her and hung up the phone. He had a intense feeling in his gut that something had gone down between them that last night she was there, but for the life of him, he couldn't remember.

He checked his watch and headed upstairs to get ready for Pedro's burial. He was glad to finally lay him to rest.

He looked amongst the few people gathered to say goodbye to his friend. As he looked down at the casket sprayed with red roses, one of his homeboys from a local group, Touch of Class, vocalized Xavier's feelings. "*...How do I, say goodbye, to what we had? The good times that made us laugh, out weighed the bad. It's so hard, to say goodbye to yesterday...*".

Xavier wiped his eyes and sighed. He cried for Pedro, he cried for his parents, Stephanie and Xavier Jr. He looked up to see April lip sync a message that she needed to speak with him. He nodded. When the procession was over, he approached her.

"Glad you could make it. What's up?" he asked as he placed a grateful kiss upon her cheek.

"A situation you ought to know about."

"What of?"

"LaShey Simpson," April told him.

Xavier pulled her off to the side and told her to walk with him. April began to explain Trey's visit to her office the week before and watched as Xavier's face began to crumble. "Her *mother?*"

"Yes, one Vivian Simpson."

Xavier placed his head in his hands. *No wonder she hasn't been to work! She thinks I set up her mother.*

He looked to April. "But you know it wasn't like that."

"I know and I explained that to Tranesha, but she's a hot head and I don't know if she believed me or not."

Xavier walked off to the side to gather his thoughts. Why was this bothering him so? He'd sat with her, had pizza and listened to her about how much she'd missed out on so much with her mother.

He played back that day inside the courtroom when her mother was sentenced. His eyes had drifted to the older, caramel complexioned woman holding the then young teenage LaShey in her arms as they cried for Vivian. *So that's where I know her from, that's where she knows me from!*

It had hurt his heart to see the young girl cry for her mother that day but he was too wrapped up in his own pain. He had just lost his wife and son a few months back while being on this very business trip Vivian was now being sentenced for.

"Damn, how could I have not known? Why didn't Doug uncover this?"

"How could you have known, Xavier. I know you, don't go beating yourself up over this. Just go and talk to her. I'm sure she'll understand." She patted him on the back and headed back to her car.

Xavier inhaled a deep breath of fresh air as he realized they had walked down to the plot where his wife and son were laid to rest.

"Tell me what to do, Steph. Tell me how to make this right. It's times like this that I miss you the most, for so many reasons." He looked to the sky. "I really need your help."

He turned to walk back to say his final goodbye to his friend. When he reached his car he thought about dialing Pebbles' grandmother again but he decided against it. He needed time to think on how to handle the situation. One wrong move and he could do more harm than good. He felt he owed her in some way. He wanted to take away her pain, bring back the years she'd lost with her mother as he wanted to do with he and Stephanie.

He'd think it over tonight, maybe go over to Sasha's and try to reach Pebbles in the morning.

••••••

Pebbles put her key in the lock and entered Xavier's home hoping to find him there. She needed to talk to him and get some things straight. Plus, she needed to tell him what she'd done. Queen refused to back out of the robberies and told Pebbles she'd better keep mouth shut because she was just as guilty as they were. Queen made it plain that if she went down, all would go down.

Pebbles' hope was to tell him, better yet warn him before it went down tomorrow night in hopes he could stop it, and he would understand. She placed the key inside the lock he had given her that Sunday afternoon and called out for him, but he wasn't home.

She felt her heart sink as she looked down on the desk and saw the autographed picture of Nelly addressed to her. "*To LaShey, good luck with finals. Sky's the limit, love Nelly.*"

Damn, that was so sweet! Her stomach became queasy as she thought of the repercussions to her decisions. *God, he's gon' kill me!*

She sat down at the desk and grabbed a stack of stationery and a pen. She figured she'd leave a note, and when he found it he could change the locks and codes at the stores tonight or early in the morning.

Mr. Winston,

This letter is hard for me write for two reasons. One is because I know about you and my mother. The other is because in attempting to trade evil for evil, I've done wrong as well. I gave Queen and Lilac the codes to the alarms at both the liquor store and the pawnshop. They are planning to rob the stores tomorrow night.

It was very hard for me to go against the only family I've known over the last five years. The Clit has been loyal to me and demands my loyalty in return.

When I heard about my mother, it devastated me and it hurt me, very deeply. I wanted to return that hurt, especially since...I thought we had something developing between us.

The night we had pizza and I came to your room to tell you I was leaving, you were draped across the bed and I went to undress you and tuck you in. I don't know why, I just did. You reached for me, you made love to me, and it wasn't until the end that you called me by your wife's name, and it crushed my heart into pieces. Then, you didn't even remember the next day at all and that doubled the pain.

So when I found out about my mother, I went crazy. I was wrong and I apologize. I pray you can forgive me and I'll except any and all consequences for my actions.

LaShey

She sealed the envelope and laid it on the keyboard of his computer. She looked around for her purse and realized she'd forgotten it at Butter and Trey's apartment. She grabbed her keys, her picture, clicked off the lights and headed out the door unsure of what the next few days would hold.

She bent over the bushes outside the front door and threw up the lunch Butter had fixed her earlier. She clutched her stomach and began to cry.

Chapter Thirteen

Pebbles' change of heart made Queen both antsy and suspicious. She called Lilac and told her the plan would go down that night instead of the next.

"I don't trust her," Queen said, slipping on her black sweats. "Call everybody and tell them be ready in an hour and meet me on the White Castle lot on Natural Bridge and Kings Highway."

When she hung up the phone she gathered her duffel bags and headed out to the car. Along the hallway, she passed Rosalyn's room and glanced inside. She was out on one of her many binges. Queen flicked off the light in her bedroom and left. *After tonight, we outta this hell hole and she's gon' get some fuckin' help.*

The codes Pebbles provided worked like a charm and the locks popped without much challenge. The liquor store was the first they hit, taking crates of their favorite liquors along with the cash in the register and night safe. Queen found the shoebox containing Pebbles' information and Pedro's jewelry. *This nigga is crazy,* Queen thought to herself.

The total came to around seven grand, including Pedro's jewelry, for which Queen figured she could get three grand, tops. The store was cleaned out and cleared in less than twenty minutes.

The pawnshop job would take longer because of the heavy equipment. TV's, DVD's, stereos and speakers were loaded into two awaiting minivans parked out back of the store. The jewelry cases were cleaned down to the wire. Queen figured all together, the pawnshop heist would bring in about one hundred grand.

Queen smiled to herself and thought of Pebbles and Trey. "Mark ass bustas", she said as she slid the gold and diamond cut Rolex on her arm, put the stolen van in drive and sped off.

••••••

Xavier returned home to eleven messages on his machine. Six were hang-ups but the seventh one quickly caught his attention:

"Mr. Winston, this is Sergeant Nielsen down at the Area II police station. I need you to come down to the station as soon as possible. We responded to two calls for burglaries, one at Xavier's Package Liquor, and one at Winston's Pawn and Jewelry, both belonging to you according to our reports. Gimme a call at 555-1414. Thanks."

Xavier dialed the desk sergeant and listened as it was again explained to him the damage done to his businesses.

"The funny thing is," the sergeant began. "That neither alarm sounded. Either they were turned off or never turned on. That's kind of strange though for both locations, don't you think?"

Xavier knew where he was going with that question--insurance fraud. Did he pay someone to rob him so he could later collect the insurance money? Xavier told the officer he'd be down to the North Patrol Station within a matter of minutes.

Xavier headed down to the station to file a formal complaint. Then he drove to each site to assess the damages in person. One of the officers on the scene told him a neighbor reported seeing a young woman driving the getaway car, a white minivan reported stolen earlier that evening from the Moline Acres sub-division.

Xavier's jaws tightened. "The alarm?"

"Didn't make a sound. It's not torn apart either. Locks were professionally picked though. My guess is the intruders either knew the codes," he looked strangely at Xavier. "Or one of your employees forgot to turn on."

It felt like deja vu to hear him say that. *Twice in one month? Employee?* Xavier's pulse began to race as he thought of Pebbles and her crew.

He quickly handed the officer a business card and jumped in his car. He headed for the part of the city Pebbles told him The Clit was from to see if he could find any of the girls and question them.

"One wrong answer and I swear...if they fucked with my shit, I'm killin' all them hoes!"

Chapter Fourteen

Queen and Lilac parked the stolen SUV along with the van behind the dimly lit warehouse on Compton and Spring Avenues. The warehouse was often used by The Clit and their parent gangs, The North Side PG's and PGL's, as a storage place, mostly for chopping up stolen cars and things of that nature.

The small abandoned former auto shop garage sat back off the street and was well hidden from the public's view, especially the police.

Queen banged on the garage door to make sure no one was inside. She loved all her homies, but this score was hers and hers alone.

She felt as if she deserved this one and she wasn't bound to share it with no one other than the participating parties.

When she got no answer, Queen pulled the keys from her pocket and opened the pad lock. The keys were only issued to the head of each branch of the NPG's. That way, if anything came up missing from the warehouse, a meeting of all the leaders was held and once the group found out who was responsible for the theft, the leader of that person's gang was held liable for the debt. It was a way for the leaders to keep a much needed tab on all the soldiers' side activity.

Queen whistled to Lilac that it was safe to begin unloading the stolen goods and went outside to help her. They stood admiring their work as the other two flunkies they had tagging along on the job did most of the work.

"You think these crack heads gon' snitch on us?" Lilac asked Queen.

She was down to do anything to help anyone in crew, but Lilac also knew that her constant run ins with the law was causing a lot of pain for her mother, Shirley. Yet, her loyalty to The Clit often outweighed common sense with Lilac.

She failed to understand that loyalty, *true* loyalty as a friend, sometimes meant going with your own mind and going your own way. Being co-dependent upon one person or a group of people to ensure your own happiness was not friendship either way. Rather, it was a control issue that Lilac couldn't see. As long as she felt that she was apart of something, whether good or bad, she was okay.

"Naaww," Queen answered as she inhaled the blunt. "Crack heads can be some of the most reliable people as long as you remain good to them. Besides, the last place a clucker wanna go is jail. They afraid of detoxin' too much. They ain't tryin' to be sick and shit," Queen laughed.

"Well, lets check 'em anyways before we let them go. Check their pockets and make sure they didn't take any extra payment," Lilac said.

"Ah, fo' sho! Aey, aey, Craig, let me holla at you fo' a minute."

The dark-skinned, one hundred and ten pound man with no teeth came hurdling over towards Queen and Lilac.

"Good job, homey. You moved them goods outta them stores with the quickness. Check this out. You know better than to stick any of them jewels in yo' pockets, right?"

"Aw yeah," the man answered.

"That's right, 'cause you know them teeth won't be the only thing missin', nigga," Queen said, patting the frail man on the thighs, checking his pockets.

"Now you know I don't play around like that, Queen. I been knowing you and your family since you was knee high to a puppy. I would never cross you like that. We like family. Plus I know you gon' take real good care of me."

He smiled and showed his checkered teeth, and Lilac couldn't help but to fall out laughing.

"You know we got that good candy for you, O.G.," she said reaching down into her pocket. She pulled out the small plastic bag containing about fifty or sixty pink and white tiny pills of boy (heroin). Lilac dumped ten pills into her palm and then handed them to Craig. "Don't use 'em all at once, nigga, and then come cryin' back for more. Make 'em last, Craig, you hear me?"

He shook his head.

"Tell yo' boy to come on over and get his present too."

"Aey, Craig," Queen called. "Aey, this shit right here goes to the grave with yo' ass, right?"

"Aw, baby, you know it. You might as well super glued my lips shut together," he said as he trotted over to his friend as happy as a kid in a candy store.

Hmm, that's a thought! Queen chuckled to herself.

The girls slapped each other a high five. Queen leaned back up against the van and pulled out her cell phone as Lilac served the other carrier. Queen dialed Trey's number and smirked to herself. *Didn't think I could pull ghetto shit off without yo' ass, did you?*

Queen wasn't calling Trey to invite her to come and partake of her newly found wealth, she was calling to gloat and brag about it, plain and simple.

"What it do!" Trey answered.

"We did it, nigga! Now, I know you didn't appreciate the way I got the info from your girl, but fuck all that! Nigga, that shit is over and dead. We got mad loot, liquor and jewelry from that nigga's spots. I told you, Trey, I told you I was gon' get that muthafucka, didn't I?"

Trey sighed an irritated breath and put out her blunt. Queen's call had instantly blew her high.

"Nigga, you missed out on hella paper."

"And it never occurred to you and 'Tonto' over there that my muthafuckin' cousin is now in conspiracy with this shit? That she could go down with ya'll asses for this and she wasn't even there? You really couldn't be that damn dumb to think he won't know she gave ya'll them codes."

"Fuck you mean? How the hell he gon' know we the ones who got him? I know I ain't gon' tell him," Queen said, getting angry at Trey for trying to rain on her parade. "Hell, anybody could've jacked his ass. This is the STL, baby. This ain't nothin' new around here. Besides, that nigga is hella insured. This ain't nothin' to him, for real."

"It may not be nothin' to him in the long run financially, but let me ask you somethin', Batman. Did you or Robin over there break a window, force the door open or anything?"

Queen frowned and then threw the roach to her blunt on the ground. "Naw, why would I do that? I had the codes, I didn't..."

Trey chuckled. "Did you break the glass in the jewelry cases?"

"Naw, nigga. What the fuck would I do that fo'? I just said I had the codes and..."

"Exactly! But a nigga who didn't have the codes would've done all that. Why? 'Cause he would've been in a hurry. No forced entry into anything means you had to have had the access codes, which means what? Only someone with access and opportunity could've provided them to you, which points right back to my fuckin' cousin. Common sense would've told you, Queen, we just tried to rob the nigga a couple weeks ago, and now you and Psycho over there go and hit him up with the alarm codes right after Pebbs become his maid. I keep tryin' to tell you, you do dumb shit."

Queen was pissed off and didn't appreciate Trey tryin' to school her on what she shouldn't have or should have done.

"Fuck all that, Trey! I set this shit off the best way I could. I done this! If you was so concerned, you should've brought yo' ass along fo' the ride. You sittin' there trippin' off some shit that *could* happen to Pebbles. Why don't you quit bitchin' up all the time? Like that shit at the club. We had to handle that shit fo' you. That bitch Butter got you…"

"Click!"

Trey hung up the phone and then ignored the next three back-to-back incoming calls from Queen. She was gettin' hotter by the minute, thinking of the effect Queen's greed could have on her cousin's life.

Trey returned her cell phone to its holster as East-Bay pulled up behind her Caddy in front of Trey's apartment building.

••••••

Queen hurled a wad of spit on the ground as Lilac asked her what Trey had said on the phone. Lilac knew Trey was going to be pissed.

"Fuck that bitch! She always think she the only one that can do some gansta shit like this. She just mad 'cause we popped this lick with out her ass."

"Yeah, but what exactly did she say?"

"What the fuck you care so much for? You scared of Trey? Just 'cause that bitch think she a man, don't mean she ball like one."

"That ain't it. I just wanna know what she said," Lilac said lighting her cigarette. She really was concerned about Trey and Pebbles' feelings. Lilac didn't like what was happening to her crew. The division was causing major conflict between them. Trey was keeping her distance and so was Pebbles. Lilac didn't feel as though they as tight as they used to be.

"She ain't talkin' about shit. You know all she worried about is Pebbles givin' us them codes. But you know what I say about that?"

"What?" Lilac asked.

"Fuck her! What ever happens to Pebbles' ass is what Uncle Sam calls a casualty of war, except in the 'hood, she's a casualty of the grind."

Queen noticed the look of shock on Lilac's face and quickly retracted her last statement.

"I mean, ain't no need fo' her to be worried about Pebbles. Ain't nobody gon' find out what happened and can't nobody prove she gave them codes to us anyway, feel me? It'll all be cool once Trey's hot headed ass cools off."

Lilac hesitantly shook her head.

"But, until then, let's go count all this money, girl!"

Queen and Lilac headed over to the door, and before stepping inside, they checked to make sure no one else was around. Queen locked the garage door from the inside and began counting the money that could end up costing them their most prized possession, their friends.

••••••

Xavier rolled down Natural Bridge Avenue looking for the deep gray colored Cadillac he saw parked outside his home the day Pedro was shot. It was the day Trey had gone to talk to Pebbles about Xavier's drug business. It was also how Xavier knew Pebbles had lied to him about the Girl Scouts she said were at the door selling cookies that afternoon.

Xavier figured Trey was just checking on Pebbles and that was the only reason he didn't push the issue about Pebbles lying to him.

Xavier had Trey's real name from the arrest report, and with Paul's help, he now had an address. As he sped down Natural Bridge passing Fair Avenue, he spotted Trey leaning up against the trunk of her car talking to a young rough looking Jamaican fellow.

Xavier rode right past them at first because he didn't want to put Trey and the unknown young man on alert to his presence. He made a U-turn at Vanderventer Avenue and parked his blue

Navigator on the opposite side of the street from East-Bay and Trey. He cut off his lights, sat back and inhaled a deep breath. *Nigga's just won't let me leave this life behind,"* he mumbled to himself as he reached over to the glove compartment, took out his nine-millimeter handgun and cocked it. He placed the gun down inside the waist of his blue jean shorts and exited the vehicle.

He couldn't believe the balls these girls thought they had. It wasn't enough for them that he had let Trey and Pebbles off the hook. But they had the nerve to come back and disrespect him and his property a second time. To Xavier, that was like a slap in the face, a bitch slap at that.

You won't get this shit off a second time, he said to himself as he awaited a clear path to cross the street. As the road cleared, Xavier began to slowly jog across the street. He didn't want to alarm the two. He knew all to well from their last meeting that Trey stayed packing a Glock as well, and from the look of her company, Xavier was sure he was too.

As Xavier approached, Trey saw him out of her side view and instinctively reached for her piece, as did East-Bay. Xavier followed on the draw and there they stood, all three with their guns drawn and aimed, Xavier's at Trey, and both Trey's and East-Bay's aimed back a him.

"Aey, homie, fuck is all this?" Trey said moving a few steps closer to Xavier.

"You know what the fuck this is! You and yo' lil' bitch ass friends robbed my stores. I know it was ya'll lil' plastic asses. Now where's my shit?"

"Look, nigga. First of all, look around you. You down here in my 'hood. Who the fuck do you think you are, comin' on my turf, drawin' pistols and shit? Second of all, you got it all wrong 'cause I don't know what the fuck you talkin' about. I ain't been no muthafuckin' where near yo' shit."

Xavier cocked his head to the side and sucked his teeth. "Bullshit! Try again."

"Nigga, not that I owe yo' ass an explanation, but you got the wrong one. I been right here hollerin' at my people all night. Ain't that right E-Bay?"

East-Bay bobbed his head. "Damn right you have! Man, you need to let me shoot this mark ass nigga fo' comin' down here thinkin' he all hard and shit."

Xavier stood tall and didn't flinch. "You do what you gotta do and I'll do what I gotta do," Xavier said, staring Trey directly in the eyes.

"Look man, I know we tried to hit you once, but do you really think I would put my baby cousin back in a bind again? Especially after you let us both go? Now, I'ma say this one mo' time, I don't know shit about yo' stores and neither does she. We can end this like adults or we can end this like *Scarface*. Which do you prefer?"

Xavier and Trey maintained direct eye contact as Xavier thought back and heeded the words of his father: "*An honest man will always look you directly in the eyes. A liar will shift his eyes from side to side.*"

Trey never broke eye contact with Xavier and he felt she was somewhat telling the truth. She may not have participated herself but she knew something. Yet he couldn't prove it so he stood down, un-cocked his nine and lowered it to his side.

Trey responded and did the same. Then she told East-Bay to follow suit. "It's good, homey. I'm sure Mr. Winston here knows he made a mistake comin' at me like that, ain't that right, Mista Winton?

"So help me God, if I find out you lied to me, I'll be back, and trust me, you won't wanna see me."

Trey smirked and waved him off with her nine.

"Man, gon' with that bullshit. You don't scare me. You should know that by now. I ain't got yo' shit, homey. Conversation over!"

Xavier turned and headed back to his car. He listened behind him for any movement of the gun pins, but none came. Xavier returned to his car and waited for his heartbeat to calm down. He glanced across the street once more to find Trey still standing, staring at him and peeping his every move inside the car. Xavier started the car and placed it in drive. *If she wasn't involved, then how else did they get into my shit undetected? Where would they get the codes?*

There was only one other way, and Xavier knew exactly what it was.

••••••

Pebbles sat on Xavier's couch waiting for him to come home. She'd heard the news of the robberies early that morning. Her grandmother had told her he called earlier yesterday to see why she hadn't been to work, so Pebbles figured he was at least willing to hear her out. But that was before Queen and Lilac took all his shit.

Her heart twisted in knots as she heard the door open and close behind him. When he turned the corner to drop his keys on the desk, she stood. Immediately he reached for his gun. Her eyes popped open and she gripped her fingers.

"I can...I can explain," she nervously began.

Xavier walked over to the phone and began dialing the number to the Area II station. Mid-dial, he threw the phone against the wall, shattering it when it landed. He walked over to Pebbles, nine pointed and began yelling at her with such fury, she thought she'd die right there on the spot.

"I told you not to fuck with me, right? But naawww, you and yo' bitch ass friends jack me anyway. After I spared you and yo' cousin's ass in the first place, you cross me? Do you know who the fuck I am? Do you know who the fuck you fuckin' with? Huh? Do you?"

Pebbles broke down and sobbed uncontrollably.

"Uh-uh, no bullshit tears. You was buck enough to take my shit, twice, be buck enough to handle the consequences."

"I'm sorry!" she finally spit out. "I'm so sorry. They had told me about my momma and I couldn't believe it was you who took her from me. I..."

"How the fuck was I supposed to know that was *yo'* momma, LaShey? I did what the fuck I had to do to maintain. I didn't handle that shit personally, my attorney did. You know the one, the one I let talk me into this bullshit with you. You fucked me, LaShey. and I asked you not to do that," he told her as his thumb found the pin to cock back the gun.

She screamed out to him, "I only gave them the access codes. I didn't take anything!"

"Bullshit!"

"I didn't! I swear I didn't. Me or Trey, we weren't there. I even came here last night."

"Last night? For what? What, my stores wasn't enough? What you come here for, to hit my crib again? Put my fuckin' keys on the table."

Pebbles was frozen and didn't respond.

"Put 'em down!"

It was his feelings for her that ultimately fueled his anger towards her. How could she betray him? How could he have betrayed himself by falling for her--allowing his thoughts to become a slave to her.

Pebbles placed the keys on the table and stood paralyzed in fear. "Xavier, please, let me explain. I care about you, I really do. I didn't..."

Xavier looked at her, her words caught him off guard. *Care?* He tried to fight the empathy he felt building within himself for her. His heart wouldn't allow him to hurt her. He lowered the gun and took a deep breath. The room stood silent as Pebbles was thanking God he'd dropped his gun to his side.

"Get the fuck outta my house!"

"But I left a..."

"Get...the...fuck...out...my...house, LaShey...NOW!"

His voice tone told her he meant business. She rushed past him and opened the door.

"By the way, just 'cause I didn't shoot you doesn't mean you're free. I will be alerting the authorities."

Pebbles nodded her head and closed the door behind her. She stood outside the front door and once again hurled over in the bushes. Her life as she knew it was ending. College, her future, all of it. All because of some "bullshit" loyalty to a clique that used her like a dish rag and threw her away. She wished like hell she'd listened to Trey.

Xavier plopped down on the sofa, popped two of his pills and gulped down the Hypnotic straight from the bottle. He stared at the phone on the floor. He thought of the fear he saw in her eyes and wanted to take it back. He wanted to forgive her once again but he couldn't. Couldn't let this pass. She had betrayed him twice, and a third opportunity would never present itself.

The phone blurred in his vision as the mixture of liquor and pills lay him out on the couch, giving Pebbles the blessing she would soon come to appreciate more than life.

Chapter Fifteen

Pebbles hung up the phone as Trey walked back into the room with a glass of water for her. Butter had a towel to her forehead trying to comfort her. "I knew I should've killed his ass," Trey shouted.

"Trey, calm down, he just yelled at me. Wouldn't you have done the same thing if not worse?"

Pebbles refused to tell Trey that Xavier pulled a gun on her. One of them would've been dead by now.

"Still, who that nigga think he is? First you come in my 'hood actin' all hard and shit, and then you get all up in my peoples' face. Aw, hell naw."

Butter rose and went to Trey. "Please calm down, Trey. She's hurt enough. She don't need this right now. She really liked him."

Trey peeked over Butter's shoulder and frowned. "Liked him?"

Pebbles swallowed her water and hesitantly nodded her head. "There's something else," she said, sitting up on the bed. Butter put her hand on Trey's chest. "Maybe you oughta let me handle this alone, baby."

Pebbles insisted she stay. "She'd find out sooner or later."

Trey definitely didn't like the sound of that.

"I'm pregnant."

"What!" Trey fumed. "Pregnant? By who? That nigga?"

"Trey, stop it!" Butter yelled.

"Yeah, Trey, by Xavier."

Butter hung her head as Pebbles began to cry. Trey sat down on the bed with her head hung low.

"What? He take advantage of you? How the fuck did this happen? What about college? I mean, we had big plans." Trey felt the tears well up in her eyes. She shook her head and reached over to the night stand.

"I'ma kill that nigga!"

"Trey," Pebbles cried. "It's my fault, not his."

"Your fault! How?" Trey asked.

Pebbles told Trey of the night she was with Xavier, that he was drunk and didn't even remember being with her. She told her of the letter she wrote to warn him, but Queen pushed up the date after she asked Queen to drop the plan altogether. She had found out she was pregnant that same day.

"I Begged Queen not to do it, but it didn't matter to her."

Trey didn't know who she wanted to hurt worse, Xavier or Queen and Lilac. She was upset with herself more than anyone. She should've never let Pebbles come along with them on any type of illegal job. Should have left with Pebbles the day she was so upset in the park. Instead, she had gotten all caught up in not being able to find Butter that day.

"So, what are you gon' do Pebbles? I got your back financially, you know that. You wanna hit the clinic or what?"

Butter shook her head "no" to Pebbles.

"Butter, I can't have a case over my head pregnant. This is what's best. I'm going to jail, Trey. What am I gonna do? What's gonna happen to me?"

Trey hugged her tightly as she broke inside her arms. "I'll take care of it, Pebbles. Trust me. But we gotta handle this situation of yours first."

Butter went into the living room and returned with the Yellow Pages. With her and Trey at her side, Pebbles made an appointment for the following evening for an abortion.

Trey removed the Yellow Pages from Pebbles and held her hands. "I'ma take care of this, no matter what it takes, you hear me? No matter what it takes. And it's gon' take money, so I gotta go."

Pebbles grabbed Trey's wrist. "And do what?"

"Just let me do this, Pebbles. I ain't gon' let nothin' happen to you, I promise. You gotta trust me, blue?"

Pebbles released her arm and wiped her face. "Blue."

Trey grabbed her gun and headed for out. "Don't let her leave here, a'ight? I'll be back soon."

"Trey," Butter whispered. "Please be careful. I know you, so please think it through first, that's all I'm saying." Trey kissed her and headed out the door.

Butter returned to Pebbles and sat down beside her. Pebbles looked over to the window. "You knew, didn't you?"

Butter nodded her head. Pebbles began to cry harder.

"He was so mean, Butter. I thought he was gonna kill me. He wanted to, I know he did. I saw it in his eyes. He obviously didn't read my letter but it doesn't matter now. I got what I deserved. He'd given me a second chance and I let Queen manipulate me. I blew it...I blew us!"

She looked to Butter. "It was gonna happen between us Butta, I felt it." She collapsed into Butter's lap.

Butter silently said a prayer. She couldn't fathom the reaction she would've gotten from Trey had she ended up pregnant by Jayson.

As they cried together, they both silently prayed for miracles--miracles to help them out of the situations that lay ahead.

••••••

After Trey left East-Bay's house to pick up the money she was owed, she sat back on the bench in Walnut Park. She lit up a blunt and thought of her life in the 'hood. What she was about to do went against every principal and 'hood ethic she lived for. But as she thought of Pebbles and the way Queen disregarded the rules and the bylaws of the crew, she frowned. *What the fuck happened to all in or all out?*

A lesson she'd learned from her father came to mind. He told her one day, sitting on the porch of the house they once had on St. Louis Avenue: "*Trey, in life, people are one of two things. They're either useful or useless. Everybody has an ulterior motive for wanting to be in your life. It could be a good one or a bad one but everybody has one. Always remember that.*"

Queen's motive was greed, at the expense of anyone, including her family. Trey couldn't let that slide. She let out a deep breath, took a swig of her twenty-ounce Bud Light and placed a call to the Area II station. She anonymously provided the names of those responsible for the robberies. Her plan was to get Queen and Lilac off the streets, get up enough grip for attorney for Pebbles and arrange for her to turn herself in a couple days after the abortion. By then, she could post Pebbles' bond and Pebbles could still take her final exams.

Trey wondered where Queen would've have taken all that stolen property. Maybe, she had it at the old building they use to meet at downtown. Trey made a mental note to check it out once Queen and Lilac was off the streets.

She looked down at her watch. She'd been in the park for four hours. She inhaled another pillar of smoke when Pebbles called to tell her of the news on the television concerning Queen and Lilac.

"Is this your work?"

Trey exhaled and felt a tear roll down her cheek. She had always given undying loyalty to her 'hood and The Clit, but what did they give her in return?

"They fucked with me when they fucked with you. Just hang up and let me handle this. You don't know shit, a'ight?"

Pebbles hung up the phone and looked to Butter who already knew the answer to the question Pebbles asked. "This can't be happening."

••••••

Xavier lay next to Sasha in bed. She'd awakened him after hearing the news of the capture of the girls responsible for robbing his stores. His head was pounding and he couldn't get his vision or memory straight. When had he left home last night? As his eyesight cleared, he realized he was home, in his own bed and Sasha was there also.

He jumped and quickly turned up the sound on the TV. He listened for Pebbles' name but there was no mention of it. As soon as the segment ended, he turned to Sasha.

"How the hell did you get in my house?"

"I called last night and you were mumbling something about you being to hard on me and yelling at me and you'd like me to come over and talk it out."

I must've thought she was LaShey, he thought to himself as he sprang from under the covers and felt relieved that he was still clothed from the waist down.

He went into the closet, picked out some clothes and headed for the shower. When he returned to the room, Sasha was still lying in the bed. Xavier threw her clothes on the bed. "Sasha, I got shit to do. You need to get dressed."

She stuck out her lips and snapped, "Why can't I just stay here 'til you get back, honey?"

Xavier shot her a look that needed no explanation. Sasha arose and quickly began to get dressed.

As she exited the house she passed Butter on her way up to the door. She sneered at Butter and threw back her head. "Maids dress like that these days?"

Butter stepped back and put up a finger to Sasha. "I don't know, does hair weave look like carpet these days?"

Sasha grabbed her head with both hands and stormed off to the car.

"Country bitch," Butter mumbled as she turned to see Xavier standing in the doorway.

"You lost?" he asked, trying to remember where he'd seen her before.

"No, I'm not lost. I came to see you, Mr. Winston. I'm Leslie, Pebb...I'm a friend of LaShey's. I need to speak with you."

"Ain't nothin' to talk about," he said as he placed his key in the lock."

"She's pregnant," Butter blurted out.

"So?"

"She's pregnant by you and she's gonna have an abortion in about two hours if you don't stop her."

"Lady, you got the wrong nigga. I don't know what LaShey told you but if this is her way of getting out of the trouble she's in, I'm..."

"The night you got drunk and woke up the next day naked. The night you two had pizza together. You slept with her. I know that because she would never lie to me. I know you mad..."

Xavier looked at her and shook his head. "Naw, naw, you got it wrong."

"If I'm so wrong, why didn't you use the gun you pulled out on her yesterday?"

Xavier fell silent. That gut feeling he'd had was right all along. *Pregnant!*

"So, why didn't she say something?"

"Oh, I don't know. She probably would've somewhere between 'Put the gun down' and 'Please don't shoot me!'. She left you a note on your desk the night of the break-in." She was now on the porch talking to Xavier face to face.

"She had gone to Queen and tried to talk her out of robbing you. Tried to explain that she was just mad about her mother and wasn't thinking straight. That she cared about you. But Queen said she would go through with it anyway so Pebbles came over to warn you and left you a note."

Xavier thought back to his episode with Pebbles yesterday and remembered her saying something about her coming over. He placed the key back inside the lock and opened the door. He walked over to his computer followed by Butter. There on top of the keyboard Xavier saw the small white envelope addressed to him.

His heart tied in knots as he read her letter and her feelings. He felt so bad for blowing up at her yesterday. Hadn't he done things in his life before without thinking? He felt even worse for not being able to remember making love to her. And now she carried his child--a child she was about to kill in a few hours.

"The police will be looking for her soon. I don't want her in that cell again, not in her condition," he said.

"She's at the house with Trey. If we hurry..."

"Lets go!" Xavier said hurrying to the front door. In an instant his heart gripped tightly as he glanced at the picture of him and Stephanie. He'd broken his promise to her. "When it all makes sense to me, I'll explain it baby."

He closed the door behind him, jumped into his Benz to follow Butter to her apartment.

••••••

Queen and Lilac were denied bail because they were already on bail for the first burglary. The charges now increased to robbery in the second degree, larceny and grand theft auto for the stolen minivans. They were each assigned a public defender at their bail hearings. April was Trey's connect and that left Queen and Lilac on their own.

When Lilac called her mother, she refused to get her bond again or an attorney. She had already put up her home less than a month ago. She prayed and asked God to give her the strength not to run to her daughter's aide this time. She needed to change, and as hard as it was for Shirley to leave her there, she had to. It was time to love Lilac with tough love.

••••••

The public defender told Queen that their arrests came through an anonymous tip. Queen sat back in the corner and thought of Pebbles. "That bitch crossed us," she said to Lilac. "She felt bad fo' that nigga and she crossed us."

She was furious. She ranted on for quite some time until she picked up the payphone and had someone three-way her to Trey.

"Yo' bitch ass cousin ratted us out. What's up with that bitch?"

Trey spit out a wad of gum from her mouth and lit into Queen. "Pebbles ain't did shit. I told you not to fuck with them stores, I told you. I told you not to fuck with me or my family. I told yo' bitch ass you'd wish you used that Glock the day in the park. This is blue, bitch, and ain't no punks here."

Queen beat the phone up against the wall. "You turned me in, Trey? How you gon' disengage from the crew like that? We go back too muthafuckin' far, bitch!"

"Fuck the crew! That's what you said about me, right? Fuck me? Well fuck you, Queen!" Trey said, before hanging up the phone.

Queen instructed her cousin, Crystal, to redial the number.

"That bitch is goin' down too, just like you. Don't forget I got mad respect in the 'hood," Queen yelled to Trey.

"And how you think you got that fuckin' respect? I put the work in to get that respect for you, and you fuck me? Yeah well, boot up and wipe yo' self off, bitch, 'cause you just got fucked with no Vaseline! Feel the blood yet?"

Trey cut the cell phone off as Butter came through the front door.

"Trey? Trey, can you come in here please?"

Trey entered the room and paused mid-stride when she saw Xavier standing behind Butter. “What the hell you want?”

Xavier raised an eyebrow and chuckled. “Look here, Sista Souljah! I came to talk to LaShey, not you.”

“Yeah, well she ain’t here. She’s at the clinic, thanks to you.”

Butter stepped in front of Trey. “You need to chill. He’s here to help.”

“Help what? He ain’t help enough by knockin’ her up? Why the fuck you bring him here, Butta?”

“Because he’s the father of her baby and he has a right to know what the hells goin’ on. They got some shit to work out whether you like it or not.”

Trey looked at Butter, enraged. “How you find him anyway? You went to this nigga’s house?”

Xavier turned to the door. “Look, I’ll find her myself. I ain’t got time fo’ this shit with G.I. Jane.”

“Nigga, what?” Trey said, lunging at him.

Xavier just smiled. “Buck if you got the balls!”

Trey paused and thought of Pebbles. If she got into it with Xavier or hurt him, it would only hurt Pebbles more. She turned to Butter and said, “That’s fucked up, Butta!” She left and went into the bedroom, slamming the door behind her.

Butter went over to her purse, took out a piece of paper and handed it to Xavier. “Here’s the place. Good luck, and hurry!”

Xavier thanked her and headed out the door.

Butter walked into the bedroom to have it out with Trey. “You think you’re so tough with this ghetto shit. I’m tired of it, Trey.”

“Yeah, well I was this same ghetto bitch when you got with me.”

“Because I thought you had potential, Trey. I thought you’d get over this ‘hood shit and want something better for your life. You’re so busy tryin’ to run Pebbles’ life, yours is falling apart right before your very own eyes and you can’t see it.”

Trey stood in Butter’s face. “I see it. I see you disrespectin’ me by goin’ to that nigga’s house today. I see you clownin’ me by still havin’ contact with that nigga Jayson.”

Butter became lightheaded. *How did she know about Jayson, and how much does she know?*

“What? You think I don’t know, Butta? You think I don’t know you fucked him fo’ ten grand? Yo’ boy got a big ass mouth and this is my muthafuckin’ ‘hood. Nothin’ gets by me.”

Butter’s eyes filled with tears, which Trey dismissed and continued to tear into Butter. “What? You couldn’t trust me to get you through school? You couldn’t believe in me? I’m out here on the grind like crazy to get you and Pebbles asses through college and what? She gets knocked up on me and you...you play me!”

“I do trust you, Trey. I just figured this ‘hood shit would get you into some trouble you couldn’t get out of and I’d be stuck.”

“Stuck?” Trey went over to the ten-by-thirteen picture of her and Butter on the wall and removed it. She punched through the plastic overlay and when it fell to the floor, she reached inside the wall and retrieved the stacks of cash.

"Stuck? You see this? You see it? I ain't stupid by a long shot, Butta. This is the product of robbin', stealin' and maybe even killin', baby. All to get you and Pebbles the fuck out of this fucked up ass city. You think this is a game I'm playin'? My shit is blue, Butta. Yeah, I'm a bitch without a dick but I got mo' heart than eighty percent of these nigga's in the 'hood. Heart to do what I gotta do fo' those I love. Heart, Butta. And you just broke it!"

Trey grabbed the duffel bag from the closet and threw some clothes inside. She packed the stacks of cash and threw one on the bed. "Get the wall fixed. I'm out!"

Butter threw her arms around Trey and screamed for her not to leave. Trey dropped the duffel bag and tried to wrench Butter's hands from her neck. "Butta, let go!"

"Trey, don't go! I'm sorry, Trey! I can make it better. Please don't go!"

Trey pulled and pulled but Butter's grip was a death lock. Trey pulled her nine and put it to Butter's chest. "Get yo' fuckin' hands off me!"

"Go ahead, shoot me Trey. I'm not letting you go. I'll die without you anyway."

Trey cocked the gun and yelled, "Let...me...go!"

Butter let her loose and Trey walked out the door. "Trey, what am I supposed to do?"

"Call Jayson."

Trey closed the door behind her and jogged down the steps to her car.

Butter rushed over to the window and cried traumatically as she watched Trey pull away.

••••••

As Xavier drove to find Pebbles, Keith Sweat put him in a daze. "*...You may be young but you're ready, ready to learn to learn. You're a little girl, you're a woman...*".

Xavier pulled up to the pink building on Euclid Avenue, parked and went inside. His insides bubbled at the thought of seeing Pebbles after he treated her so badly.

The young secretary directed him to the Family Planning Clinic on the fourth floor, and Xavier rushed to save the life of his child.

Exiting the elevator, he spotted Pebbles standing at the counter signing forms. She was softly crying. He walked over to the desk and touched her arm. She jumped as she turned, floored to see him standing there.

"Xavier! What...what are you doing here? How did you..."

"None of that matters, LaShey. What matters is I'm here. We need to talk," he said motioning for them to sit down.

Pebbles took a seat in the pale green chair and rested her sweaty palms on her knees. "You here to cuss me out some more?"

Xavier looked at her and hung his head in shame. "About yesterday, I...I apologize. I lost my head. I'm sure you can understand that. I thought you were to blame."

"I was, Xavier, No matter what reason I thought I had, I shouldn't have given them those codes. I'm so sorry."

"Me too--about yesterday, about your moms, and the night..." his words faded off as he felt his voice catch in his throat.

"It's okay, really. It happened. I was just as much to blame. I knew what I was doing, I wanted it to happen," she said.

He looked into her eyes and felt like dirt. He'd said some horrible things to her yesterday. Truth was, he cared more than he would allow himself to admit. She had stormed into his life and turned it upside down, made him feel things he thought he'd never feel again. He'd only known her briefly, but to him that wasn't important. It was impact she'd had on his thoughts and his dreams in that short amount of time.

"Are you sure you wanna go through with this?"

Pebbles lowered her eyes and blinked back her tears. "Don't you want me to?"

Xavier looked away as he thought of his promise to Stephanie and his heart was torn. The thin-framed nurse appeared from the hallway and called for Pebbles. She gave him a final glance and got to her feet. She walked towards the nurse feeling as if she wanted to die.

"No!"

Pebbles turned to the voice. Xavier came face to face with her. "You won't kill my baby. I lost one, I won't lose another."

"Xavier, we can't..."

"We can and we will. I'll figure this out but I need some time. This can't go down like this."

Pebbles felt a sigh of relief as she turned to the nurse and told her she'd changed her mind. The nurse and said, "That's just fine with me. Good luck, sweetie!"

Pebbles thanked her and turned to Xavier. "So, what now?" she asked.

Xavier gestured towards the hallway. "We go somewhere and sit down to talk. We'll handle this."

He opened the door and placed his hand on the small of her back. She felt a relief deep down inside her that he'd come and stopped her from getting the abortion.

Once they exited the building, they were met by two plain-clothes detectives. Pebbles' stomach tied up in knots as they approached. Xavier stepped in front of Pebbles as if to protect her.

One officer stepped to the side of Xavier and held up his badge. "Ms. Simpson?"

Tears immediately sprang from Pebbles' eyes as she softly answered, "Yes."

Xavier wrapped his arms around her waist. "She's not going anywhere with you. Those were my stores. I own them and I'm not pressing charges against her."

The second detective took out his handcuffs. "That's not up to you, sir. The DA has issued a warrant and we have to do our jobs and bring her in. Anything past that, you gotta take up with the DA."

The tall, burly detective grabbed Pebbles' arm and Xavier put his hand in the officer's chest. "Aey man, you ain't gotta grab her like that, she's pregnant. Don't manhandle her."

His partner, a small framed white man, took out is handcuffs and warned Xavier, "We can take you both if you'd like. Back up sir. Let's not make this any harder than it has to be."

Pebbles was grateful for Xavier's assistance but she didn't want him getting into any trouble himself. She'd caused him enough problems.

"Xavier, please, don't argue. I can't handle you getting into trouble too. I have to go with them. I made this mess, I gotta clean it up."

The officer cuffed her and led her to the car. An all too familiar scene hit his heart as she again mouthed the words to him, "I'm sorry." Only this time, he knew it was true.

His mind raced with a thousand thoughts and his emotions got the best of him. At that moment, he realized he wanted her. He wanted her and only her. She was the one he could lavish with all the love that Stephanie had left behind in his heart. He had to help her. He'd do anything and everything he could to get her out of this mess and he knew just who to call.

He placed the call to April and told her he needed a favor and would pay any price to get to it done.

Once he explained it to her, she laughed. "This shit gets more and more bizarre as the days go by."

She told him she'd get right on it, and if she couldn't get the DA to reconsider the charges, she'd at least get her out on bond.

Chapter Sixteen

April was unable to work her magic enough to get the charges dropped against Pebbles. The DA was up for re-election and wanted to make an example out of the girls.

She got Pebbles bailed for fifty grand cash or property. Xavier put up the money and was there to pick her up from the station. Pebbles was so glad to see him but couldn't help but wonder why he would go out of his way like he had to help her.

"It's simple; stress on you means stress on our baby. I lost one, I'm not planning on losing another one," he told her.

Her feelings were visibly hurt and Xavier fought within himself to be truthful with her. He still loved Stephanie, still longed for her, missed her. But he also wanted a chance with Pebbles.

"That's not totally true. I don't wanna see you mess up your life, not like this. You deserve better than this. I don't know, maybe I feel like I owe you this because of your mother," he lied again.

"You don't owe me anything," she said, wishing he would just go and leave her be. She knew he felt something for her by the way he acted at the time of her arrest. *Why does he always have to act so damn cool?*

"Thanks anyway for getting me out of there. But I really should be getting home. I don't want to worry Trey or Nana any longer."

"Your home is with me now. At least until this is over. April called and explained to your grandmother that your job was now a live-in position. That way she wouldn't worry. She'll take you to get your clothes and things. I'll be at the house waiting for you."

"Live-in? My Nana went along with that?"

"She sure did, after a little convincing."

"Why are you doing all this?"

"'Cause I coughed up fifty grand and I need to make sure you don't run off," he smirked. He placed his hand underneath her chin and told her he was kidding and everything would be okay. He would do what he could.

April led her off to the car as he stood and watched them disappear. He knew what his next move had to be.

••••••

Queen lay back against the wall and smiled at the news that Pebbles had been arrested.

Lilac felt differently about the situation, and for the first time made her opinion known to Queen. "I can't believe you ratted her out like that, Queen. That was fucked up!"

"Me? What about that bitch, Trey, rattin' us out? I know you didn't think she was gon' get away with that shit!"

"You right, *Trey* fucked us, not *Pebbles*. We got what we wanted from her. You didn't have to handle it like you did. You on some extra shit now and I ain't with it."

Queen was amused by Lilac's rebellious attitude. She rose to her feet and stood within inches of Lilac's face. "So what? You got treason written on yo' heart now too? What, you bad now? You ain't shit! You a flunky, unable to think for yo' self, fend for yo' self and handle shit by yo' self. You ain't nothin' without The Clit."

Lilac stepped back feeling the nail Queen just pierced through her heart. She had given all to prove to Queen that she was worthy of being a soldier. She was crazy about Trey, and although she didn't care too much for Pebbles, she wasn't down for rolling over on her.

Lilac lived to be loyal to The Clit but Queen had showed her true colors and snitched. No color Lilac would paint across her heart. True, Trey had crossed them, but Lilac figured Trey had done it to save Pebbles.

"What, Clit Queen? You messed that up. Look around you, ain't nobody here but us. There is no crew, they all jumped ship 'cause of you and yo' greed. And guess what? I may not be nothin' without you, but from the looks of this orange jumper, I ain't shit with you either. I may have been yo' flunky, but not anymore. I'm out too. You can have this shit!"

Queen's temper rose quickly at Lilac's defiance. She looked around the concrete holding facility for the C.O. When she didn't see one, she called Lilac out to step into the bathroom. "You want out, it's only one way outta this, you know that," she said gesturing with her fists.

Lilac showed no fear. She stood still and didn't flinch. "Fuck the bathroom! Show me what you got right here, 'cause I'm just like Bone Crusher, bitch! I ain't never scared!"

A crowd began to gather in the dorm to watch the two go at it.

Queen, on the outside, claimed she didn't want to go to the hole over Lilac. "You ain't worth it, bitch. When one of these hoes is about to mop this muthafuckin' floor with yo' ass, don't look for me."

Secretly, Queen knew in her heart she was frightened of Lilac's frame of mind. Lilac felt she had nothing to lose, and Queen knew all to well that abandonment could unleash a fury that couldn't be contained.

As Lilac walked over and took a seat to watch TV, Queen sat down on her bunk and felt the one emotion she'd never felt inside The Clit--*alone*!

••••••

Xavier entered the St. Peter's Cemetery and drove down to the lot where Stephanie and Xavier Jr. were buried. He'd stopped and bought a dozen roses along the way. He walked over to the burial plot carved into an angel holding a baby in her arms. He sat down on the grass in front of the statue and rested his head back against the stone.

His heart ached for letting them go, but he felt that Pebbles' child, his child, was life's way of telling him it was time to move on--not as he had been, entering meaningless relationships, constantly comparing them to Stephanie and withholding his emotions.

His eyes watered. "I know, Steph, I made a promise to you and I broke it and I'm sorry."

The tears were flowing freely. "It wasn't planned this way. It wasn't my intention to fall for her that way I did. Seeing her in that closet, in your dress stirred my heart in a way I hadn't felt since you were here. I'll never love anyone like you, Steph, you know that. You'll always be apart of my heart. But if I continue to give you all of my heart, I may as well have died with you."

"We didn't meet under the best circumstances but we met. And I know it was for a reason. Now she's pregnant with my child and I wanna be there for her, like...like I wasn't able to be there for you."

He wiped his face and lay the roses down. He stood up, removed the gold and diamond wedding band from his finger and placed it on the top of the stone. "I love you, Stephanie. I always will, but I wouldn't be the man you loved if I kept denying my heart of the one it needs. I hope you understand and I hope you will still and always be my angel."

He returned home to pack up Stephanie's things when Pebbles arrived. He'd asked Patricia to handle the disposal of his wife's things because he knew she'd see that someone special received them.

Patricia was glad to see Xavier move on with his life and she wished him all the best. Once he explained the situation, she told him, "You're always going to be my son, no matter what you do. I'm glad you found someone. I'm glad you're finally ready to move forward with your life."

Xavier smiled. "I know Ma, and I love you for that. In my heart, you'll always be my mom as well."

When Pebbles saw the boxes, she began to cry. "You didn't have to do that. I would've taken the couch."

Xavier walked over to her. "It's fine. This needed to be done a long time ago." He sighed. "I guess I just didn't wanna let them go..." He looked at her and ran his fingers through her hair. "...Until now," he said as he leaned in and placed a kiss on her forehead. He wiped the tears from her eyes. "It will be alright, I promise."

"I'm worried about Trey. I haven't heard from her. Butter hasn't heard from her either. I'm scared."

Xavier embraced her and held her tightly. She melted against his chest.

"She'll call you soon. Right now, I want you to get settled in and shower while I get these boxes to the garage. Then I'll get you something to eat. Lord knows we can't have you cookin' and feedin' my baby that mess!"

With that, he got her to smile. She walked over to her luggage and began to unpack.

Her grandmother had seemed so proud of her. *If only her grandmother knew!* She'd made some bad decisions and caused a lot of people a lot of pain, yet, here she was, moving in with a man she felt she'd never deserve.

Once she was settled into her room and had eaten the takeout Chinese food, she sat down on the sofa and sipped the glass of orange juice Xavier insisted she drink. She smiled at him and shook her head.

"What's so funny," he asked, putting on his favorite Floetry CD.

"You don't think this is a tad bit strange, me being with you, you helping me? Me having a baby with you? This is weirder than *The Young and The Restless* and *The Bold and The Beautiful* put together."

I'll admit, it is a bit strange. But," he said, pulling her off the couch. "I have been crazy about you since the first moment I laid eyes on you. It's just that I promised Stephanie when I married her that I would never have a child outside our marriage, and it was that love and that bond that I shared with her that kept me from saying this to you sooner."

"Xavier, I know how much you loved..."

"Shh, yes, I loved her very much. I always will. But I've either dreamed or thought about you every moment you're away from me and that tells me that heaven must be giving me a sign that it's okay to break that promise."

Her heart smiled and she relaxed her head upon his chest. As Floetry serenaded them, the moment became magical. "*...All you gotta do is say yes, don't deny what you feel, let me undress you, baby. Open up your mind and just rest. I'm about to let you know, you make me sooooooo...*"

With his hands on her lower back and his jimmy pressed against her body, he kissed her with all the passion he felt for her. She welcomed his tongue and dove into the pleasure headfirst. He reached underneath the pastel sun dress and entered her with his yearning.

Her soft whispers drove him crazy.

"LaShey?"

"Yes?"

"I'm gonna take you upstairs, lay you down, lick you from head to toe and live out every dream, every fantasy I've had since I first laid eyes on you. And not only will I remember it this time,

I'm gonna hit it enough to where I can replay it mentally over and over again."

AND THEN IT ALL ENDED...

Pebbles stood at the wooden defendant's table in the downtown courtroom as April pressed a reassuring hand on her lower back. Pebbles glanced over her left shoulder and made eye contact with Xavier. He nodded and mouthed the words, "I love you," and sent her a kiss.

The short, Japanese female judge began to read Pebbles her sentencing decision. The Honorable Yamasita made it known to Pebbles that she wished she could have been harsher than the law allowed in the sentencing guidelines.

"The story of Ms. Simpson and Mr. Winston, while touching, will not influence the decision reached by the court. The charges you have pled guilty to are very severe in nature in this court's opinion. You, along with your friends have shown a blatant lack of respect for the victim's personal property and the laws of this state and society as a whole. It is also my opinion that this court has been very patient and lenient with you in allowing you the time to give birth to your daughter last month. It is my opinion that this case has been drawn out for far too long."

"Therefore, this court hereby sentences you, LaShey Marie Simpson, to a confinement term of fifty-seven months in the Vandelia State Prison, with at least one third of that confinement to be served before parole consideration. Ms. Simpson, you are now remanded to the Missouri Department of Corrections to begin serving the imposed sentence. Bailiff, please take Ms. Simpson into custody. This court stands adjourned."

Pebbles felt her heart rip from inside her. *Fifty-seven months? How am I gonna make it that long in prison, away from Xavier and Zavaria? How can this be? How will they make it?*

Pebbles felt as if she was going to faint as she watched the small-framed judge walk out of the courtroom. *No! Come back! This is a mistake! I can't leave my baby. I can't leave my family. Please, come back, say you made a mistake, please!*

When the door to the judge's chamber closed behind her, Pebbles knew this was all too real. She would be going away to prison. She had followed in her mother's footsteps by going to prison and leaving a child behind. She fell down into the chair, gasping for breath. The tears flowed freely as she thought of life behind bars.

"What am I gonna do? I can't do this, I can't be away from them that long, I can't!"

Xavier ran to her side and knelt down to console her. His heart ripped in two to see her hurt this way. "It's gonna be okay. It may not seem like it right now, but somehow, I'll make it alright."

April sat beside her and gently patted her thigh. "I'm so sorry, LaShey. Believe me, I did my best."

"I know," Pebbles said.

"It's state time. We'll have you out of there in a year and a half, tops. And I hate to sound like a broken record, but sometimes things like this bring two people closer together. The story of how you and Xavier found each other and fell in love out of all that has happened is both amazing and inspiring to me. He loves you, LaShey, trust me. I've known him for a very long time and he'll be there for you. That, you can count on. It'll be okay."

Pebbles sobbed hysterically as the bailiff told her to stand. Xavier cupped her face, placed a kiss on her lips and whispered, "Don't worry, baby. You know that this isn't the end of the road for us, right? For the first time in a very long time, I want something to work more than life itself. It feels so good to need you, LaShey, to want you, but most of all, it feels good to love. I love you, baby, and I promise you I'll be there everyday that I'm allowed. Me and the baby. And we'll be right there waiting for you when you get home."

Pebbles looked deeply into his eyes. She knew his words were both heartfelt and sincere. "Blue?"

Xavier felt the tears roll down his face again. "Bluer than the ocean is blue. I'll be there."

They kissed again and Xavier watched sadly as the bailiff pulled Pebbles away from his arms and led her though the brown oak door marked "Inmates".

His tears continued to roll as Patricia and April rubbed his back.

"It's okay, sweetheart, go ahead and let it out," Patricia told him, trying to console both him and Zavaria, who was crying for her mother also. Patricia knew that Xavier was shedding tears for more than just the situation with Pebbles. It was the second time in his life that Xavier felt as if he couldn't save the woman he loved.

"But, when you're finished, be finished. And then use your love for her as the strength you'll need to be there for her and take care of your daughter. You know you're not alone in this and she needs to know that as well."

Xavier shook his head, letting his mother-in-law know that he both agreed with her and understood her. He knew what he had to do.

He'd once again made a promise to the woman he loved. He promised to be there...just as he had been there to help her and push her to ace her final exams and SAT's. Just as he was there for every Lamaze class, every appointment and finally, the delivery of their beautiful baby girl.

He was there when Pebbles had lost her grandmother to a sudden heart attack a few weeks after her graduation, and there every night when Pebbles cried herself to sleep, worried about Trey.

He was there, on September seventh, when the opening of the new Edwards Jones Dome in St. Louis brought a climax to Xavier's level of commitment to Pebbles. The halftime scoreboard lit up at the opening of the Rams home football game and read, "LaShey, I love you so much and I'd be honored to have you as my wife. Will you marry me?"

Xavier kept his promise to Pebbles and visited her every visiting day to make sure she spent as much time as possible with Zavaria. The bond between mother and child was important to Xavier and his heart glowed every time he saw them together. Pebbles kept every picture Xavier sent on the poster board above her bed so that they would be her first thought when she rose in the morning and her final thought before she went to sleep.

Patricia moved in to help with the baby while Pebbles was incarcerated. Her "grandchild" was the love of her life, and she lavished her with the love she didn't have a chance to give Stephanie and Xavier's baby boy.

••••••

One Sunday morning, Pebbles was called to the Family Visitation Center at an earlier time than usual. *I hope nothing is wrong,* she thought to herself as she scrambled to do her hair and makeup.

"Don't worry, *mami*. I'm sure that fine ass man will wait a little longer for you," the young Hispanic inmate told her. "I've been here long time and I can't remember seeing a more dedicated man. And he's fine too! You'd better hold on to that one, *señorita*!"

"Oh, I plan to," Pebbles stated, but for some reason with a degree of uncertainty. She had been gone a year now and she secretly feared that Xavier would have second thoughts about her and their life together. Even though he had been so dependable all these past months, Pebbles was so use to the negativity she had grown up in, she subconsciously was expecting something to go wrong any day.

I really gotta work on that shit before I get out of here. Now, get it together girl, yo' future husband is waiting for you.

Pebbles entered the gray door to the all glass Family Visitation Center after being searched. She scanned the room for the man she loved and the daughter she felt so blessed to be able to call her own.

Mid-way, she noticed a very familiar face. With braids hanging mid-back level, face clear and perfect, with a navy blue Sean John sweat suit on, was Trey.

Pebbles ran to greet her at such a pace, the CO thought she was about to attack Trey and instinctively reached for her club.

Trey stood to embrace Pebbles and gripped her so tight, she thought she'd break her ribs.

"Trrreeeeyyy! Ooh, Trey! Where have you been? I've been so worried about you, I thought something had happened to you."

Trey released Pebbles and gripped her hands inside her own and stepped back to take in every inch of her baby cousin. "You look amazing, Pebbs! I missed you so much. I'm so glad to see you. I'm glad to see you doing a'ight and things are going good for you."

Pebbles smiled and began to cry. Tears of joy rolled down her cheeks as she embraced Trey once again. "Oh, Trey, I'm so glad you alright. I have spent so many nights awake thinking about you, wondering..."

"I know. Sit down, let me talk to you," Trey told her, taking a seat in the orange cushioned chair beside her.

She exhaled a deep breath. "This has been a long time comin'. I know you've been worried sick about me and shit and I'm so sorry fo' that. But fo' a minute Pebbs, I was so lost out there. I mean, I really didn't know who I was anymore after all that shit that went down. That night, after I made that call, I hated myself. I felt like… like not only did I turn them two bitches in, I felt as though I turned the entire 'hood in. You know I lived and died for the 'hood and loyalty. I became one of the people I despised most in life. Pebbs, I became a snitch, a rat. And, in doin' so, I told on two bitches I use to call my best friends for years. Not only that, but I didn't think of the trickle effect it would have on you. I should have known Queen wouldn't let you be.

"You always depended on me to take care of you and to look out for you and I failed. Fo' that I deeply, deeply sorry. I didn't, I never..."

Trey paused.

"It was never my intention to see you in here, word is bond, you know that. I just wanted them hoes to know that fuckin' with you meant fuckin' with me."

Pebbles put her finger up to Trey's lips. "Shh, Trey, that shit don't matter to me. You know that I know you would never purposely hurt me. You practically raised me with Nana and I love you! No one or nothing can ever change that."

Trey hugged Pebbles tightly and placed a kiss on her neck. She appreciated Pebbles' understanding and forgiveness, but she still had heaviness on her heart. She slumped back in the chair. "So, you did Nana good at her funeral, right?"

Pebbles hung her head and sighed. "Yeah, she looked real nice too, Trey. Them Fosters did her real good."

"You know why I didn't make it, right Pebbs? I mean, you understood, right? Everybody that's still down with Queen was expectin' me to be there."

Pebbles shook her head. Silence fell between them for what seemed like hours, each engulfed in her own thoughts.

"I loved her, Pebbs, you know that. And I love you too. But after that shit with Butter fuckin'..."

"You talk to her?"

"Naw, naw I can't. Can't even bring myself to look at her. She hurt me, Pebbs, more than I thought I could be hurt, feel me?"

"Yeah, I feel you. But Trey, aren't you that same person who just sat here and told me how sometimes, we don't think of the trickle effect our choices have on those we love? Butter loves you, more than anything in the world, you know that. She just got scared with the life you was livin'. I can understand that. She became unsure of her future with you and began to wonder if one even existed for you and her as a couple. She made a mistake,

Trey. We all did, but those mistakes don't have to be the end of the road for us."

Trey smiled at Pebbles, admiring the woman her little cousin was quickly becoming. "Yeah, I hear you. Maybe one day I'll give her a call. Anyway, enough about me. They treatin' you right in here? You ain't got no static with nobody do you? Nobody better be fuckin' with you."

"Naw, it's good. I pretty much get along with everybody in here 'cause I don't be on all that drama and bullshit. I got one goal up in here, and that's to get the hell outta here. I do everything and anything positive I can to make this time go by faster so I can get home to my daughter and my man."

Trey shook her head. "I still can't believe you and that nigga is gettin' married. You know that shit was all over the news, right? The odds of that shit!" Trey said, laughing.

"Tell me about it. I still can't believe it, Trey, but he's so good to me and he takes excellent care of me in here, and Zavaria out there. I couldn't have prayed for a better man."

"Just goes to show you, things really do happen for a reason," Trey responded.

"Yep, they sure do."

"Look at you, growin' up on me and shit."

She grabbed Pebbles and held her tightly.

"Mind if we share that hug?" Xavier said, standing over them and holding Zavaria. They were dressed alike in powder blue Phem sweat suits, with Zavaria sporting the matching scrunchie around her bushy ponytail.

She was eighteen months now and growing more and more every time Pebbles laid eyes on her.

"Of course you can," Pebbles said, standing to greet them both. She planted a slew of kisses on her baby girl and a major one on her father. "Hi, baby!"

"Hey, beautiful!" he responded, handing Pebbles the baby.

Pebbles hugged Zavaria and turned to Trey, who was now standing behind them.

"Trey, meet your baby cousin, Zavaria."

Trey smiled and took Zavaria by the hand. "You are so adorable. I'm Trey, your auntie, although, I'd really appreciate it if you never call me that."

They all laughed in unison. Pebbles glanced over to Xavier. "Don't Trey look great, baby? I can't believe I have you all here together in the same room at the same time."

"How you doin', Trey?" Xavier said, extending his hand to her. "It's good to see you again. I wish it was in better circumstances, but that's okay."

"It's blue, man. I know what you mean. Aey, uhh...I just wanted to say, thanks. For taking care of my lil' cousin and making sure she's blue. Her," Trey said, taking the baby from Pebbles. "And my gorgeous lil' cousin here."

"Well ya'll, lets go outside and enjoy the weather," Pebbles insisted.

"Naw, you two go ahead. I know you both have a lot of catching up to do. I'll be fine. I'll just chill here and read a couple of magazines," Xavier assured her.

"You sure, baby?"

"Yep, now go."

"You're the best."

"Only 'cause I have the best," he said kissing her softly on the lips.

Pebbles escorted Trey over to the gray metal picnic table outside in the visitation yard. The flowers were beginning to wither because of the fall weather, but all in all, the yard was still beautiful.

Trey, Pebbles and Zavaria took pictures by the garden of roses that landscaping inmates had planted and grown. Pebbles promised to send a copy to Trey when they came back from the outside lab.

"So where are you staying?"

"Around. You know I'm gutta, baby. I can chill anywhere," Trey said pointing to the door. "Let's go back inside. Zavaria's cheeks are starting to feel like popsicles."

"A'ight, but then you gon' tell me why every time I ask you somethin', you change the subject on me."

As they entered the door, Trey stopped Pebbles and stared at her. She was truly proud of Pebbles and wanted so badly for Pebbles to be proud of her too. *I got major things in the works,*

Pebbs. I wanna tell you but I can't. But just wait. Yo' big cuz is definitely gon' set if off.

"Aey, Pebbs, I'm happy fo' you. You got a good thing goin' here with my man in there, and I'm proud of you for embracing the opportunity to be happy despite the odds. You went fo' broke and I like that in you. I got mad respect fo' you fo' that. You got a nigga...my bad, a *man* that really loves you, a beautiful baby girl and a bright future ahead of you."

Pebbles hugged Trey as tightly as she could with Zavaria between them. She whispered to Trey, "So do you, Trey. You just have to embrace it too."

••••••

Shirley sat on the full sized brass bed, packing up the last of Lilac's things. She had decided to donate them to the Salvation Army. As she sat and scanned the room, she thought of all the memories she and Lilac had shared in that room. Early on, the road had been rough between them but as time went on, Lilac and Shirley had become the best of friends.

She walked over to the dresser, picked up Lilac's sixth grade picture from the mantel and smiled. In six pigtails and a pair of huge red framed glasses, her child's future looked so promising. Her face looked so pure and innocent, as if life hadn't come to corrupt her yet. But it had, and Shirley knew it all too well.

Shirley hung her head and silently cried. *Where had I gone wrong? What happened to my little girl?*

Shirley could vividly remember the day she was forced to accept her suspicions of the horror Lilac was suffering at the hands of her drunken ex-husband, Randy.

In her early years, Lilac was a happy-go-lucky, typical nine year old little girl, full of sunshine and joy all the time. Yet, little by little that seemed to change the more her ex-husband came around. Lilac didn't like him from day one. It was a saying of the old folks that if a child doesn't like someone, there's a very good reason for it. Lilac would always run to her room when he came home, and she would remain there until he left.

Shirley's maternal instinct told her that something was wrong. She could feel it, she just wasn't strong enough to question Lilac about it, and certainly not fearless enough to confront Randy.

Randy was an evil man, and when he was drunk he was three times as evil. The beatings he laid on Shirley were neither provoked nor deserved. They came unexpected at first, then more frequently and more violently.

The blood-filled bath water she came home to and found Lilac soaking in let her know that Randy's evil wrath had moved to another level--a level involving her baby girl.

Shirley was overwhelmed as she stood at the entrance to the rose pink and white bathroom, seeing her little girl sitting in the tub, bleeding from between her fragile thighs. Shirley hesitantly walked over to the small ceramic white tub and lifted Lilac's face to hers.

"Lilac… Lilac, baby, what happened to you? Who did this to you?"

Shirley knew the answer already. She just needed to hear Lilac say his name.

"No one. No one did it. I fell and hurt myself. I was playing on the broken bicycle in the yard and hit a big bump."

Shirley knew that wasn't true, and she knew Lilac was afraid to say it was Randy who had hurt her. She too was afraid of Randy, but she was a grown woman. She could defend herself. Lilac was her only child and no mother, no sane mother, would want to see her child tortured. Shirley would see to it that Lilac wouldn't go through the same horror she experienced from her perverted uncles and older cousins.

"Lilac, baby, look at me."

Lilac raised her sorrowful eyes to meet her mother's.

"Baby, I know that's not what happened. Momma needs you to tell me who hurt you like this."

"I said I fell! And what you gon' do any way? You can't even stop him from hittin' you!"

Lilac rose up and hoped out of the tub, splashing the bloody water on Shirley's face and clothes. Lilac snatched a towel and stormed to her room as Shirley sat on the bathroom floor, crying her eyes out.

She wanted to call the police, but if Lilac wouldn't tell her the truth, Shirley knew that there was nothing the police could do.

Lilac shut her out completely over the next few days. She wouldn't talk, she wouldn't eat, she wouldn't go to school and she wouldn't leave her room.

Three nights later, Shirley came home from work to find Randy lying on the brown stained carpet in Lilac's room, next to the bed. He had a knife wound to his lower chest, his pants, unbuttoned and his shirt torn and soaked with blood. Lilac stood over him, knife in hand, with a deranged look on her face. She was naked from the waist down.

"I knew he'd come back. I sat in this room until he did. I was waiting for him. I knew you couldn't keep him out the house so I waited. I slept with a knife under my pillow. He was never gonna hurt me again."

Shirley stood in fear. Lilac's eyes were glossy and cold. No tears were falling. She was solemn and stiff. Shirley slowly walked towards her, looking at Randy lying there with his eyes open and bleeding all over the place.

"Lilac, honey, give me the knife. Give momma the knife."

She reached for the weapon and Lilac's fingers were locked on it as if she expected Randy to wake up from a deep sleep. Shirley cautiously moved closer and grabbed Lilac's hand. As she pulled the knife from Lilac's hand, she pulled her close her.

Shirley squeezed Lilac tightly and apologized to her for not being there to help her.

"It doesn't matter, Momma. I took care of myself," Lilac told her as she looked down at him and hurled a wad of spit at his face.

The day in the tub would be that last tear Lilac shed. She refused to cry anymore, and a sharp blade became her best friend. She refused to let anybody hurt her again.

She had loved The Clit because she felt protected, as if no one could harm her because her crew had her back, something she never felt her mother had after that day.

Lilac was a loyal person, and if she felt close to you, she would fight to the death for and with you.

As Shirley taped up the last box, as hard as it was, she thanked God for answering her prayers. She wanted Lilac to be safe. Her anger was so elevated after Randy, Shirley really felt that Lilac would hurt someone soon.

In prison, Lilac had hooked up with some of her old clique, The Switchblade Sistas, in the facility she was sent to. Always about proving herself, Lilac took up some beef that wasn't hers and paid for it with her life.

Living long enough to ask God for forgiveness and accept Jesus as her personal Lord and Savior, she was saved...*her soul was saved*!

The tears streaming down Shirley's face weren't tears of sadness, for Lilac was finally, at peace, at rest and above all...*safe!*

••••••

Butter sat in the mahogany chair of her Biology class at Southeast Missouri State University in Missouri and awaited the arrival of her instructor. It was the first day of her second semester of her sophomore year of college.

She had spent the last year and a half, trying to get over Trey. The first few months brought a mountain of stress and had been the hardest for her.

Butter couldn't imagine herself or her life without Trey. She would lie awake at night, praying Trey would come walking through the front door. She refused to sleep in the queen-sized waterbed they once shared and made love in countless numbers of times.

Often Butter found herself jumping up and running to the smoked gray glass window in the living room every time she heard the whopping bass of a car passing by, hoping it was the woman she loved.

Butter would dial Trey's cell phone number, wishing she would answer, but if she didn't, Butter began being content just to listen to Trey's voice on the answering machine. Butter's messages were long in length at first, pleading with Trey to give her another chance, apologizing profusely for betraying Trey and sleeping with Jayson.

She understood that for Trey, a straight lesbian, Butter cheating with a man was the ultimate betrayal because of the way two women made love to one another. The closeness, the intimacy and the exchange of bodily fluids made lesbian love making extremely personal.

Although Butter comprehended that, she tried through her messages to make Trey see her point of view, her side of the story. She wasn't asking Trey to excuse her behavior, but understand the things that led up to Butter making the mistake in the first place. Butter pleaded and pleaded but to no avail…still no response from Trey.

Soon, the fact that Trey pretended as if Butter didn't exist made her furious, and Butter's messages became bitter. When you hurt in life, you feel as if the other person should hurt as well. Regardless of whose at fault, no one wants to hurt alone. Butter wanted Trey to feel her pain, so her last her message became both insulting and hateful.

It took Butter all of four months to realize and accept the fact that Trey wasn't coming back. It was their third year anniversary and Butter truly believed in her heart that despite everything, this would be the day Trey would call for their special day. She was wrong.

As the days turned to nights and Butter's heart could take no more, she had decided she had to let it go. She ran a hot bath, lit a slew of vanilla-scented candles around the tub, put on their favorite Ruff Ends song and cried Trey out of her system until she could cry no more.

"*...Maybe you've been waiting for the man from all the fairytales, or maybe just the man from all your dreams. Try to think reality, explore the possibilities, 'cause girl you know you've waited for so long, for some one to love you...*".

The next morning, Butter awoke with a new attitude about love. She still loved Trey deeply and a part of her still wanted Trey to come back home, but Butter had finally accepted the reality that it was over between her and Trey.

Butter walked into the brown and white checkered kitchen and reached into the closest to retrieve a trash bag. She walked back into the bedroom and began gathering all the things Trey had left behind months ago and Butter didn't have the heart to throw away. *She'll be back,* she kept telling herself.

Slowly, Butter placed the clothing, teddy bears, music CD's, shoes, cologne and other things inside the trash bag. Then a sudden wave of second thoughts swept across her heart. She reached down inside the bag and pulled out her favorite fragrance Trey possessed. She sprayed a cloud of Eternity into the air and inhaled the scent as deeply as she could. *Damn, I miss you!*

She lay the bottle beside her on the bed. *Well, maybe I'll just keep this one thing.* One thing turned to many as she found herself unable to get rid of the memories of happier times. She bundled up the photos and placed them inside a Nike shoe box and set it atop the closet shelf.

As Butter set the trash bag at the front door, her cell phone rang. She knew the ring tone all too well.

"Hey, Butter! Any word yet?"

It was Pebbles. She had called off and on, worried sick about Trey. Butter knew Pebbles was dealing with a lot of things going on in her own life, but Butter held some unwanted resentment towards Pebbles. She felt as if this whole situation was Pebbles' fault, that if Trey hadn't constantly run to Pebbles' rescue, she'd still be home.

"No, no word yet, Pebbles. I'll call you if I hear somethin'." With that, she ended the call. Her cell rang back immediately.

"Yeah, Pebbles?"

"This ain't Pebbles, Ma. Where you been? You ain't been callin' a nigga. What's all that about? You still got things to do to make good on my investment, and you need to be gettin' at me, like soon," Jayson told her.

"Look, Jayson. You never said this was more than a one time thing. I thought that was what it was, and that's it."

"Come on, Ma. You know me better than that. I put a lot of money in yo' pocket and I expect my investment to come back to me tenfold, you feel me? Get it together. I'll be through there in an hour."

"You can't just come over here like that," Butter insisted. You know Trey..."

"Is gone," Jayson interrupted. "That he/she ain't been there in months. I made sure of that."

"What you mean you made sure of that?" Butter asked, looking down at the phone.

"I made sure she knew how good I fucked the shit outta you that day. Made sure that word got back to her, letting her know that she couldn't steal you from me and think she was gonna get away with it, and think I wasn't gon' hit that again."

Butter sat down on the couch, feeling sick to her stomach. *So that's how she found out! This lousy muthafucka!*

"Why you do that, Jayson? Was your pride really worth all that? Was frontin' to yo' boys and boostin' yo' ego worth destroying two people's lives?"

"One person's. Yours will still be intact, *if* you're ready in an hour."

He hung up the phone and Butter sat there furious. *I hate this bastard! But the fucked up part is I need him to get through school. The money he gave me won't last through the first year and I got moving expenses and shit. Damn you Trey!*

Butter rose from the couch and headed to the bathroom to shower and get ready for what she knew would be a night filled with Jayson humping all up and down on her like a dog.

The relationship lasted through the end of her first semester at SEMO and then she'd had enough. She was tired of feeling used up. She changed dorms, changed her number, and swore that she would make it on her own, by any means necessary.

The slim young white girl behind her tapped her on the shoulder and handed her a small white piece of paper. Butter thanked her, smiled and opened it. Her eyes frowned as she read it's contents.

Damn, you fine! You got a man?

Butter snickered and balled up the paper. No, she didn't have a man, and hell no, she didn't need one. Jayson had dogged her body enough.

The second note came.

Why you play me like that? I just wanna know if you're free, ' cause I'm still diggin' you. In fact, I can't get you outta my mind. In fact, I'm in love with you.

She laughed at that one, then it met the same fate as the first.

Love? What was it really all about? She'd thought she'd found it with twice in life: One, she left--the other, she fucked up.

She tried to concentrate on the teacher as the tap came on her shoulder for the third time that morning. She turned around irritated to find Trey sitting behind her, smiling at her. She looked great, her hair braided crazily and hanging mid-chest level, and her skin smooth and radiant.

Butter's emotions were running rampant. Part of her wanted to throw her arms around her and kiss her right there in class, the other part wanted to spit in her face.

Trey held up another note and opened it. "Let's leave. We gotta talk and I got somethin' to show you."

Butter hesitated, thinking of all the hurt she suffered in the past eighteen months. She turned back around in her seat and faced the teacher.

Trey whispered, "I really need to talk to you, Butter."

"I'm in class, Trey. And I'd appreciate it if you left."

"Butter..."

"No, Trey."

Trey exhaled a deep sigh. She rose from the seat and walked towards the door with Butter's eyes glued to her. Butter wanted to run after her but she fought the temptation. She had finally let her past go, and talking to Trey would only rehash old feelings--feelings that seemed to take forever to let go of.

Through the rest of the class period, she couldn't focus. All she could think about was seeing Trey--her face, her smile, the emotions that rushed her when she lay eyes on her. But most of all, the hurtful feeling she still got watching her walk away again.

After class, Butter rounded the corner towards her English Literature class to find Trey standing at the door waiting for her. Butter's heart jumped as she approached her.

"Butter, I'm not leaving until we talk."

"What is there to talk about Trey? It's been over a year. When I wanted to talk, you weren't interested, so why should I be interested now?"

"Because I was a fool," Trey told her, touching her arm.

Butter moved away even though Trey's touch felt so damn good to her. Butter walked over to the guardrail looking out over the campus yard. Trey followed her and touched her on her lower back.

"You know, Trey, when you first left, I didn't think I would live without you, I didn't think I could. I counted the days, the hours, the minutes and even the seconds at first, but then the crying stopped. And guess what, Trey? I got through the seconds, the minutes, the hours and soon the days without missing you. I don't need you now, Trey. I needed you then."

Trey looked away from her and then back into Butter's eyes. "You hurt me, B, and I can't tell you how that felt. You, out of all people. I would have never thought it would have been you."

"Trey, I made a mistake. I got scared and I..."

"That's just it, Butter. You got scared of being without me, of losing me but then, you go and do the one thing to make me leave you. I don't understand that. And with that nigga, of all people," Trey said, gripping both of Butter's arms. "Do you know how it felt to have that nigga callin' my phone, tellin' me what kind of underwear you had on that day? Vicky Secrets that I bought you. Braggin' about how he knocked yo' back out. How deep he went. Places no dildo could reach. I knew the same damn day, but I wanted to see if you would be loyal enough to at least tell me. 'Cause if it really was a mistake, I felt it would eat at you and you'd break it down to me. But you didn't. And that hurt the worst. Then all that shit with Pebbs and Queen. All that shit got to much fo' me and I had to get away befo' I killed somebody, and I didn't want it to be you."

Butter stared at the ground and for the first time since the ordeal, accepted responsibility for her actions. "I'm sorry I hurt you, Trey. God knows I am, and believe me, I've been paying for it dearly over the past year and a half. It's been hell for me. I've just begun to get my life back on track and now here you are. What am I supposed to do? What do want from me?"

Trey stretched out her hand. "Come with me and find out."

Butter looked into Trey's eyes and fell in love all over again. She enclosed her hand into Trey's and followed her out to the parking lot.

At the car, Trey pulled Butter close to her. "I know I hurt you more than you deserved. I just was lost and I didn't know how to cope with being involved in a situation I couldn't control. You know me, I'm used to handling mines, and when I things started going down hill, I felt a snowball effect of negative shit involving those I love most in life. I couldn't handle being helpless. I'm gangsta, baby! Nothin' comes my way I can't handle, and when it did, I nutted up. I apologize fo' that. I forgave you, though. It took Pebbs to wake my stubborn ass up and show me I was fuckin' up."

"Pebbles!" Butter asked, surprised.

"Yeah, I went to see her a few months back and met my new lil' cousin, Zavaria. She's holdin' in pretty good. Got a good man by her side and that's what made me realize I wanted that. I want what she has. I missed you, baby, and I love you. And believe me, you can't get no bluer than I am right now."

"Oh, Trey, I love you too!"

Butter wrapped her arms around Trey's neck and kissed her deeply and passionately.

"Now, come with me. I got somethin' to show you."

Trey drove her to a location blindfolded, and led her out of the car. She stood behind her, wrapped her arms around her waist and told Butter to remove her blindfold. Butter began to jump up and down, screaming in excitement as she stared up at the ghetto style writing on the sign that read "Trey B's Cuts & Thangz."

The St. Louis style barber shop sat in between Mimi's Beauty Supply and Crazy Jay's Clothing Store. Trey had the place hooked up with a California theme and STL colors blaring red and white.

Butter grabbed her and hugged her tightly. "How did you do this?"

Trey backed up, turned Butter to face her and smiled. "I wanted to be near you while you went to school, maybe get a second chance to work on us. And, aey, nigga's at college need they shit cut too."

"But, I thought..."

"I know what you gon' say. It's not the 'hood. Well, baby, the 'hood let me down and I had to make a choice: Save what I love or be a lonely, dumb muthafucka that let love pass me by. I chose to seize the opportunity," Trey said as she smiled and thought of Pebbles. "I said 'Fuck it'! I love you, baby, and I don't have to be in the 'hood to keep it gangsta."

Butter wrapped her lips around Trey's and whispered, "You'll always be gangsta to me, baby."

"Blue?" Trey asked.

"Bluer than blue!"

••••••

Queen sat at the tan painted metal visiting room table in the Oklahoma State Prison, awaiting her visitor. She had moved to the Oklahoma facility for constant misconduct in the Missouri prison.

Queen's 'hood mentality always made her think she was untouchable. She was used to girls bowing down to her. Used to making examples out of those weaker than her and those who chose to test her. But of course, Queen soon found out that the other female inmates in the system was just as gutter as she was. Queen had only reigned in the 'hood because she had a crew that was down to put in work and had her back, right or wrong.

Yet she had now alienated all her friends and was now forced to stand on her own two feet. That, she soon learned inside the walls, was easier said than done, and although she stood her ground, she was quickly taught the hardest lesson she would have to learn inside the prison system: "Don't write a check yo' ass can't cash."

The most recent incident, where she mistakenly landed a blow to a CO's face, landed her in the hole for three months while she awaited a disciplinary transfer to a higher security leveled institution.

The smaller-framed inmate had grown tired of Queen's constant pushy ways and decided Queen had pushed her to the limit.

One evening after a long day's work in the outdoor garden, Queen had begun her usual taunting of the young girl about the Laclede Town set she claimed back in "The Lou."

"Bitch, yo' 'hood ain't shit. I'm running out of fingers tryin' to count the number of hoes we beat down from yo' 'hood," Queen said, walking three girls behind the inmate.

Queen had collected a crew of weaker inmate groupies that broke out in laughter as Queen cracked on the young girl.

The inmate, all of 5'1, turned to Queen and blurted out, "You know what bitch? I'm so fuckin' tired of you always talkin' that bullshit about what you and yo' weak ass crew did. From what I hear, it was yo' crew that snitched on yo' ass and put you in here. Don't sound to me like they give too much of a fuck about you. And for you to be *Queen B*, yo' name ain't been called for a visit since you touched down. So miss me with that bullshit, bitch. We both standin' here crew-less, so what you wanna do?"

Queen felt the stares from her fellow inmates as they awaited her response. Full of so much hate and fury, Queen lashed out at the young girl, hitting her on the right side of her jaw.

"Bitch, you betta recognize where I from!" Queen shouted, swinging a bevy of punches at the girl's head. Beating her down however, was not in the cards.

The young girl moved swiftly and threw a combination of blows to Queen's face and head, causing Queen to start bleeding from the mouth.

The CO's ran over and began slinging inmates right and left, trying to get to the volatile inmates.

When a big black female officer grabbed Queen's left arm, Queen swung around her right arm and landed a wild punch against the guard's head.

Queen was slung to the floor, cuffed and escorted to the tiny concrete cell known as the hole.

As she sat there in the middle of the floor staring up at the paint peeling from the ceiling, she played back the words that had burned her soul over again in her mind. *From what I hear, it was yo' crew that snitched on you and put you in here.*

How could Trey do me like that? She called herself down? I *was there when she had nothin', when she was broke and beggin' on the corners for change to feed her and that lil' bitch, Pebbles.* I *made her belong.* I *made the 'hood respect her dike ass. And this is how she repay me?*

Queen felt the tears roll down her face as she scanned over all the graffiti on the dingy concrete walls, all the sets represented in the facility. Her eyes locked on one in particular. The engraved writing spoke volumes to Queen. She scooted closer to the wall.

"It doesn't matter how many stand behind nor beside you in a war, it only matters how many remain there when the war is over."

Queen lay back on the uncomfortable green mat and cried. She was alone and it was all her fault. *No one understands. It always been about everybody else. What about me? Who gives a fuck about me? Nobody, but I'm supposed to care about everybody else and their life. They don't care about me. My daddy's MIA (missing in action), my brother left me and I ain't gon' get started on my momma's ass. She never cared about nothin' but men and dope. Shit, I'm gutter, I gotta look out for myself.*

The walls Queen had built around her heart and emotions seemed virtually impossible to break through. She had grown up feeling abandoned and unloved. Underneath all the tormenting of those weaker than she, was the need to feel important, needed to feel superior. She needed to see the fear in someone else's eyes other than her own.

But at that moment, the words once again flashed across her mind: "*It only matters who remains...*"

The answer was simple--no one. Her greed and feelings of being inadequate her entire life had driven away the only people who actually cared about her--her crew.

As she sat at the table, dressed in her facility issued, freshly starched uniform, she nervously twiddled her thumbs. Queen couldn't imagine who would be coming to see her. She had been down almost two years of her fifteen year sentence without even a word from the 'hood or any one else. She pretended that didn't bother her, but secretly, Queen felt forgotten and that hurt.

She watched the mid-sized woman approaching, and Queen almost fainted when she recognized who the visitor was. Rosalyn had gained weight, filled out and looked healthy...she looked clean!

Queen wanted so badly to hate her for the way her life had gone thus far, for the impact Rosalyn's drug addicted life had upon her. But with all that had happened, Queen couldn't help but feel a little happy to see her.

Yet when Rosalyn reached her, Queen folded her arms and sneered at her. "What you doin' here?" she asked Rosalyn as she took a seat across from her. Queen admired the long, full length of Rosalyn's now pretty hair and the beauty of her face along with the classy Gucci outfit she wore.

"I came to see you."

"I know that much. I can see that. For what, is what I wanna know. What made you finally come by here? I been gone almost two years now. What, you finally remembered you had a daughter? And why you come up in here dressed like that? You got a rich smokin' buddy this time, huh? Man, you gotta be kiddin' me."

Rosalyn reached across the metal table and touched Queen's hand. Queen jerked away and placed her hands down on top of her lap.

"No, sweetheart. I don't do that anymore. I'm clean, Natasha, and I know that may be hard for you to believe, but it's true."

"Yeah, right."

"Yeah is right. When you left this time I went down. So far down I didn't think I could ever get back up again. I was always use to you being there. When I realized you were gone, I started using twice as much. I mean, I was out there so bad, I was beginning to do any and everything to get high. Just trying to escape from everything. I was truly at the bottom of the barrel.

Then a man, a good man, walked into my life and got me some help. He directed me to a center that was willing to stick with me until I won the battle against drugs. I fell a few times but what mattered was that somehow I found the strength to get back up again.

Finally, I was able to stand on my own two feet. I've been clean ever since and I...I got a job, can you believe it? A good paying job. And guess what? I got us a house. It's not fancy and it needs a little work. It's ours and it's away from that neighborhood that has made things so bad for the both of us."

Queen shifted in her seat. "Why you telling me all this? What makes you think I care? I'm in a cage for ten plus years, or can't you see that. I don't have a home. This concrete facility is my home. I can't believe you! Now you wanna clean up and act right. The main reason I did this crazy shit was so I could get you some damn help," Queen said, banging her fist onto the metal table.

The CO started in their direction and held up one finger to Queen to let her know she had been issued a warning. Her next disturbance would cost Queen her visit.

"Now you wanna be in my life," Queen continued. "Now you wanna be a mother. When I needed a mother, you were too busy chasin' behind some broke down, run over pimp. All you wanted to do was go clubbin', smoke weed and sleep with every man you thought could keep getting you high. I mean, it would have been different if you were gone all the time because you were working late hours, trying to build a better life for Ron-Ron and me. But naw, you were off in them streets just tryin' to do you and that's all you cared about was you, not Ron-Ron or me, just you."

"Do you know how many times I could've landed up in this hell hole, out there in them streets just tryin' to keep a roof over our heads? That wasn't my job, Momma, it was yours. Somewhere down the line you forgot that. You either forgot it or you just didn't care."

"I got tired of fendin' for myself and not havin' shit to show for it. So I pulled this stupid job, hoping to hit a lick big enough to take care of both of us and get you some help. But these last couple years have made me realize that nobody cares about me but me."

"Do you know what a damn slap in the face it is to be the one who always helped everybody else? Always the one who looked out fo' your peoples and then be left fo' dead when shit get twisted? I ain't got no love, not even one single word from anybody since I been in here. Not my so-called friends, my crew nor you.

So, why you here now? Oh, I get it. It's okay for you to show me some love now that you have climbed the social ladder, right? Well guess what. It would've meant more to me if you would have came up in here with yo' hair all over yo' head and strung out, rather than after you reached this new level of glamour and then decided to remember me."

"You forgot to struggle with me, survive with me. So what, now that you got all this stuff and doing good for yo'self, I'm the final wrong in yo' life you tryin' to make right? Well, gon' with that, Ma. It's too late for all that."

Queen bit down on her bottom lip to stop the overwhelming flow of emotions she felt building inside of her.

Rosalyn sighed and shook her head. She felt so defeated by her daughter's words. Her little girl had every right to be upset, every right to be angry. Rosalyn knew that pain, the pain of abandonment all too well. She to was raised by a single mother who chose the streets and men over her children, and often Rosalyn was left to fend on her own.

So like Queen, Rosalyn ran the streets in search of the love she didn't receive at home--Rosalyn in men, Queen in The Clit. Both had been disappointed and now it was time for Rosalyn to change all that. It hadn't all made sense to her until that moment, until she heard her daughter speak from her heart of the hurt and pain Rosalyn's lifestyle had caused her.

She had come this far and refused to turn around. She wanted so badly for Queen to believe in her. She reached for Queen's hand.

"It's never to late. God is a God of second chances. Sometimes, like in my case, third, fourth and fifth chances. Honey, I haven't been there for you. I wasn't there for your brother either, and baby, I'm truly sorry for that. I know I've been a lousy mother, but I was sick then. My addiction was a sickness, can't you try to understand that? But I'm better now and I'd really like a chance to make it up to you. Both you and Ronnie." Rosalyn used her fingers and wiped the tears from Queen's eyes. "A chance to be your mother."

Queen frowned and turned away. "Yeah, well I'm sorry too. You ain't here. We all outta chances, here."

Rosalyn sighed and stood to leave. She wouldn't force her. A lot of hurt was between them. Queen will come around in her own time. "I love you, honey. I hope you can believe that one day, because it's true. I really do love you." She walked over to the officer to be processed out.

As Queen watched her mother about to leave, her heart split in two. All her life she wanted to hear those words from Rosalyn. Now that she had, she was turning her away.

Queen felt the tears roll freely down her face as she remembered the words on the wall in the disciplinary cell: "*...It only matters who remains...*".

There she was, the mother she had longed for all those years. The only one who still remained beside her. No one else was left. Queen decided she no longer wanted to stand alone.

She jumped up from her seat. "Rosalyn!"

Rosalyn turned to face her.

"Will you be back next week?"

Rosalyn smiled.

"Nothing but death could keep me from it!"

••••••

The twenty-three months seem to drag by as Pebbles waited for the call to pack out the next morning. She couldn't sleep. Her mind was racing a mile a minute. Deep inside, she was thankful for the time away from the 'hood. Not to downplay the hurt it 'caused Pebbles to be away from those she loved most in life, prison had given her the time to re-think her life. It gave her the time to contemplate the decisions she had made for the sake of "belonging", and time to get to know herself both emotionally and spiritually. For Pebbles, it was time well spent to herself, preparing her to be a better person, a better mother and someday, a better wife to Xavier.

There would be a lot of women Pebbles would miss at the facility, some she wished she could take with her when she left, like the elder women who took her underneath their wings and taught her how to do time and not let the time to do her. She promised herself that she would keep in touch with each and every one of them as she hugged and kissed them before leaving the state institution.

As she exited the front sliding glass door, Pebbles inhaled the fresh spring air. For some reason, "free" air smelled so much better than "incarcerated" air.

There he stood, looking so handsome and sexy to her. Xavier was leaning on the passenger side door of the black and silver Yukon truck he had just purchased for Pebbles as a coming home present. When Pebbles saw him, she ran to him and engulfed herself in Xavier's arms.

"Hey, baby!" he softly whispered in her ear. "It feels so good to hold you. I'm so glad to see you."

Pebbles hugged him tighter and smiled. "Me too."

Xavier released her and dangled the keys to the Yukon in front of Pebbles face. “For me?” she asked, peeking around Xavier’s shoulder.

“Sure is...for you to drive back and forth to school.”

Pebbles kissed him softly and passionately. She loved him with all her heart and she was so thankful he was apart of her life. She counted her blessings as she started her new truck and began to drive away from the beige concrete facility. She stopped the truck and gave the prison one last glance. She smiled and nodded her head. This would be the first day of the rest of her life. She would attend Saint Louis University at the beginning of the upcoming summer semester. Xavier, Trey and Patricia would have it no other way. And just when she thought she could feel no greater joy than the night she returned home and went to sleep holding Zavaria in one arm and Xavier the other, Xavier gave her the gift of a lifetime.

As spring turned to summer and June 16th arrived, Pebbles stood face to face with the man of her dreams inside the Eastern Star Baptist Church.

She glanced out at the small gathering as Xavier’s first cousin, Danny, serenaded them with a love song to bless their union: “*...I’ve been so many places, I’ve seen so many things but none quite as lovely as you. More beautiful than a Mona Lisa, worth more than gold and my eyes have had the pleasure to behold. You’re my latest and my greatest...my latest, my greatest inspiration...*”.

Pebbles smiled at Patricia and Butter, then blew a kiss to her two favorite girls, Zavaria and Trey.

When the preacher asked, “Who gives this woman to be wed?” the temple doors opened and in stepped Vivian.

"I do!" she replied as she staggered up the aisle, afraid of fainting as she lay eyes on her beautiful daughter.

Pebbles looked to Xavier and smiled. The tears began to fall as Pebbles wrapped her arms around his neck. "You are so wonderful! I can't believe you did this. I love you so much!"

"I love you too! Now stop crying and go give your mother a big hug."

Pebbles lifted the train to her all crème-colored wedding gown and took off towards Vivian. Vivian too ran and wrapped her arms tightly around her daughter.

Xavier smiled at April and winked his eye. She'd come through again. He was so happy and he felt so complete. He bowed his head and silently spoke to Stephanie. *I love you, Steph. Thank you for allowing me to love LaShey as well.*

He had now brought in the last fish, and he was now blessed with what he'd always both wanted and needed...*a family!*

Other Novels

By

Allysha Hamber

Keep It On the Down Low
Unlovable Bitch, A Hoe is Born
What's Done In The Dark
Mimika Avenue

Coming Soon

Unlovable Bitch II, Redemption or Revenge

Made in the USA
Charleston, SC
12 February 2011